The Rovers:
A Tale of Fenway

Paul Ferrante

Paul Ferrante
2016

Published by
Melange Books, LLC
White Bear Lake, MN 55110
www.melange-books.com

The Rovers: A Tale of Fenway ~ Copyright © 2016 by Paul Ferrante

ISBN: 978-1-68046-242-5

Cover Art by Stephanie Flint

For the two men who made this story possible:
The late, great Robert Creamer
and
The one and only Bob "Lefty" Cremins

This one's for you.

hurt, tips had been poor that day, and on top of that, he'd promised Maria to pick up Chinese takeout on the way home. If it weren't for Clancy, he'd be long gone. Hell, this was getaway day; even the ballplayers were probably on their way out to the team bus by now to start the season's last road trip. Dom was grateful for the week he'd have off. Of course, he wouldn't tell Clancy that. The old man would say he was blaspheming or some such shit.

It wasn't that he disliked the old guy, far from it. Quite to his surprise, Clancy had welcomed him warmly when Dom had come aboard in midseason. Nobody could say how old Clancy was—you never asked—but management was aware he was slowing down and would need a replacement soon. As the senior usher, Clancy could've made Dom's life miserable, but from day one, he'd clamped onto the young Italian with the fervor of a televangelist. Besides being shown the ropes and every nook and cranny of the old park, Dom had to endure an almost daily diatribe on the beauty of baseball, the Red Sox, and Fenway, not necessarily in that order. After every game Dom would make the trek to Clancy's area behind home plate to sit and listen to him ruminate on the glories of the National Pastime as he sucked on an old briar pipe. With his faded red usher's hat pushed back on his thin silver hair, loosened tie and too-big uniform, Clancy suggested an elongated Barry Fitzgerald from the old Bing Crosby movies. He was a living legend at Fenway. Even the ballplayers, who generally regarded the stadium workers as somewhere below plankton on the food chain, found the time to talk to him.

Dom sighed as he approached the old man, whose pipe sent wispy trails of smoke skyward. He thought back to his first day on the job. There he was, a 30-year-old Guido from Little Italy, taking this job to supplement his income as a sanitation worker—the hours meshed perfectly—to ease the financial strain on his wife and three young daughters. Like everybody else in his neighborhood, he'd played some ball as a kid, nothing special. He'd followed the Sox, even traded their bubblegum cards, until cars, girls, marriage, and finally kids had pushed baseball way down on the priority list. Then, at the D'Ambrosio Christmas Eve feast at his aunt Rose's, he'd casually mentioned to his favorite uncle how his family was feeling the pinch. Uncle Carmine, a small, dark man with a perpetual five o'clock shadow, had chewed his scungilli thoughtfully, then snapped his fingers—which sent some fra diavolo sauce flying—and said, "I tell you what. I take care of Mr. Harrington's lawn. He's the guy who runs the Red Sox. I bet he could find you something there, at Fenway. Maybe a vendor, tickets, whatever. And you get to go to the ballgames!"

"Sounds good to me, Uncle Carmine," was Dom's reply.

When he'd relayed this story to Clancy that first day the Irishman had rolled his eyes. "But do you *love* it, boy?" the man had practically cried out.

"Love what, Mr. Clancy?"

"This!" the old man blurted, sweeping his arm across the bleachers out to the Green Monster. "The smell of the grass, peanuts roastin', the pop of baseballs striking leather, bats crackin', the organ playin'?" He dropped his voice to a conspiratorial tone. "Where do they play organs, boy?" he whispered.

"Excuse me?"

"I said where do they play organs, boy?"

"Church?"

"Aye," he smiled, "an' that's yer first lesson. This is a *cathedral*, boy, and you're to learn to treat it with respect, with reverence. You and I, we've got the greatest job in the world."

"Ballpark ushers?" Dom hadn't wanted to aggravate the man, but he couldn't hold his tongue. "C'mon, Mr. Clancy," he said, "wouldn't you rather be, like, a ballplayer?"

Clancy held up a gnarled hand, which now clutched a wooden match. "Yes and God bless all here," was his reply. With a flourish, he struck the match on a nearby seat and lit his pipe, smiling all the while.

That same pipe now drew Dom to the old man like a magnet. He settled into the seat next to Clancy and began, diplomatically, "Listen, Mr. Clancy, I'd like to stay with you a while but—" Then he saw the pipe, bowl side down, beginning to burn a hole in the old man's jacket. "Jesus Christ," Dom said as he swiped the pipe away, all the while looking at the Clancy's face. He was dead, very dead, his eyes closed as if he'd just nodded off. Dom started to spring from his seat to get help, but he caught himself. Lowering his butt back into his seat, a strange

3

smile came over his face, and there followed a peaceful, quiet feeling of awareness quite unlike anything he'd ever felt before. "I guess I don't have to go tell them right away, Mr. Clancy," he whispered.

He sat with Clancy for a long time.

*   *   *   *

John Henry Williams looked around at the folders and ledgers that inundated his desk and rubbed his temples. Cicadas chirped outside in the fading Florida sun, reminding him of the many days he spent fishing with his dad on local lakes and in the Gulf. Their angling expeditions had been cut back since Dad's strokes, so they were more of an occasion now. What he'd give to be hip deep in water, fly casting, instead of doing this stuff.

He forced himself to look back at the computer terminal, which flashed a spreadsheet of his father's businesses. As Dad's financial manager, he'd been given a tremendous amount of responsibility and work, especially since the illness. It seemed everyone wanted a piece of his father, even more so when word went around that maybe he didn't have too much time left. They were wrong, but Dad had slowed down, no doubt. Even Ted Williams, the greatest hitter who ever lived, was mortal.

The past few years had not been easy for them. First, a business partner had bilked his father for thousands before his eventual arrest. Then, their fledgling sports card company, despite producing an excellent product, had failed. The two strokes just compounded matters.

On the plus side there was the Famous Hitters Museum they'd opened in nearby Hernando which gave his dad a chance to meet with current and former players to talk about his greatest passion, hitting. And the money rolled in. Lord, people were paying $100 or more for an autographed baseball and hundreds more for a bat. Of course, along with this came endless phone calls concerning forgeries, rip-offs, scams and whatnot. When he wasn't flying around the country making business deals, John Henry was appearing on *60 Minutes* or being interviewed by some sports card publication or baseball show. There were times he wondered what it would be like to be the son of a bank clerk.

It was during this latest rumination that Ted Williams entered the room. Despite his cane and slightly stooped posture, he still dominated this and every other scenario he was part of. A ruggedly good-looking man in his younger days, he was America's closest thing to John Wayne, a gifted athlete and former war hero. In many ways, probably, he was more John Wayne than Wayne was himself, since the Duke was merely an actor portraying heroes. "How's the work going?" he barked in his familiar booming voice.

"Not bad. I'll knock off soon."

The elder Williams settled into a La-Z-Boy and clicked on a widescreen TV. "San Diego's playing Pittsburgh tonight on ESPN. I want to watch Gwynn hit. The kid finally listened to me."

John Henry smiled as he punched the keyboard. Tony Gwynn, the National League's preeminent batsman, had sat at the foot of his father the previous December and had been given a chapter and verse explanation of why he should be able to hit for more power without losing points off his average. Gwynn, who was pretty sharp and open to suggestion even after many stellar years in the majors, had implemented Williams' subtle technique changes and he was up around .370, with a lot more pop. The world's greatest hitter couldn't have been more pleased unless, of course, it was he who was out there hitting.

The telephone rang and John Henry picked up. He listened, frowned, and put his hand over the receiver. "Dad, phone for you."

Williams, absorbed in the game, waved him off. "I'm not here. Take a message."

"It's Mr. Harrington from the Red Sox."

"Okay," sighed the slugger, clicking off the remote. "I hope this is damned important." He took the receiver, listened, shut his eyes and slowly exhaled. John Henry heard him say, "All right, I'll catch a morning plane. See you around noon. Just make sure Yazstremski and Clemens get their asses there, too." He hung up and ran his hand through his hair. "John Henry, get us on a morning flight to Boston, I've got to be at Fenway by noon."

The younger Williams rolled his eyes. "Dad, you know you're not supposed to be traveling around too much—"

Williams Senior cut him off. "First, I haven't been to Boston since they named that tunnel after me a couple years ago. Second, there's been a death. I promised when the time came I'd be there."

Names of former contemporaries of his dad raced through John Henry's mind. More than a few were very old or sick, and it pained his father when another one passed on. "Who was it, Dad?" he asked softly.

"Clancy, Martin Clancy."

John Henry furrowed his brow. "Clancy… second baseman, Detroit?"

"Nope. Senior usher, Red Sox."

"What! You're going up there for an usher's funeral? Come on, Dad, you don't have to—"

Williams held up his hand. "I promised. We all promised."

"We who?"

"Me, Yaz, Roger Clemens. We were his favorites. We promised him that when he croaked we'd bury him."

"Can't you just send the family some flowers?"

"No. There is no family. And there's no funeral home to send it to, anyway."

"So, where's he being buried?"

Williams grinned. "That's the beauty of it. See, someone else made him a promise long ago. He's being buried at Fenway. *Under the pitcher's mound.*"

"You're kidding me!"

"Wish I was. Now, call the airlines and get us two tickets for tomorrow. I'm going to sleep. And tape the San Diego game for me."

"Wait a minute, Dad," he called to the aged slugger as he shuffled away. "Could you please tell me why this guy rates getting buried under the goddamn pitcher's mound at Fenway Park? Who the hell was he?"

Ted Williams turned back in the doorway. "It's a long story. I'm probably the only guy in this world outside of Mr. Yawkey, God rest his soul, that knows the whole thing. I'll tell you on the plane. Okay?"

"Sure," said John Henry Williams, as he reluctantly dialed the number for American Airlines.

Chapter One

Cashel, Ireland—March 1926

The day that changed the life of Martin Clancy began as most others did. His father climbed the ladder to the loft which served as Martin's bedroom and roused him from his dreams at 5 AM with a gentle shake and a "Come, boy, there's work to do." By the time Martin awoke and shook the cobwebs he could feel the damp, cold morning in his bones. Once the fire in the Clancys' thatched cottage petered out the dwelling took on a chill that pierced your soul.

Martin kicked off the heavy quilts, then pulled on his work pants and a coarse woolen sweater. After adjusting his heavy socks and boots, he was ready to face the Irish dawn. He slipped down the ladder into the main room. Dominated by a huge fireplace, it served as living room, dining room and kitchen. He took his woolen cap from its peg on the hearth and whipped it onto his head, covering his blonde curls.

He could hear his mother stirring in the curtained alcove that served as his parents' bedroom. She was pouring water from the blue pitcher she kept on the dresser into its basin. Soon she would be building the peat fire once again and preparing a hearty breakfast of porridge, soda bread and tea. His stomach growled in anticipation.

The teen stepped outside into the dewy half-light. Immediately he glanced up at the Rock of Cashel, silhouetted against the clouds. No matter where one lived in Cashel or its environs, the castle and cathedral, which until 1101 had served as the seat of Irish kings, dominated the landscape. One only had to look skyward. Somehow, its presence was comforting to Martin, and more than a few times during his workday on the farm he would stop and stare in awe at St. Patrick's Cross and the Round Tower. What kings and fair maidens had held court there? And how many brave and bold knights had pledged their allegiance between those now broken, drafty walls? The Rock of Cashel was actually built upon a hill, but the hill seemed mountainous to Martin. Brooding, foreboding. It was a place of dreams, of danger... of immortality, perhaps.

Shaking himself from his daydreams, Martin entered the stable attached to the house. He was depressed this day, as he had been for some days now, for he was fast realizing that his lot in life had been decided for him. He was 17 years old and yet he felt like a child. His mother, who at 42 seemed lifeless and melancholy, smothered him with love, protection and doting attendance. Irish mothers are typically devoted to their sons, and Martin's situation was magnified, for he was an only child. However, his father, Mike, approached life as a farmer with dogged determination and a dour demeanor that kept most people, including Martin, at a distance. The elder Clancy was humorless. He got up, worked his land, ate, smoked his pipe and went to bed, with nothing to look forward to the next day other than repeating the whole process. The highlight of his existence came on those occasions when he went into town, bought a pouch of tobacco, and enjoyed a pint of stout with his farmer compatriots while they discussed the weather and crops. Martin was not allowed to accompany his father on these trips yet. In fact, outside of grade school and the occasional church function, he'd had no social life whatsoever.

Martin hunkered down his six-foot, one-inch frame onto a tiny stool and began milking Amy, the only cow they had. Besides her and their plow horse, Dickens, the Clancys kept no livestock, only a few chickens. Their 25 acres of potatoes, cabbage and turnips kept them busy enough. The daily tasks he and his father did were monotonous and backbreaking, and the Clancys, like all Irishmen, lived with the unspeakable dread of another famine like the one that had blighted their country in the 1840s. Many had left to try their luck in the United States in the last half-century or so, but Mike Clancy would never leave. The Rock had him within its grasp.

Suddenly, as if on cue, the sun broke through and bathed the town of

Cashel in gold. The Rock of Cashel shown as an emerald, its setting the majestic hill. Even as Martin bent to his task, the castle loomed above him like a watchful elder.

After he finished milking Amy and fed the chickens, he returned to the cottage for breakfast. The main room was now aglow from the fire, and he could smell his mother's strong tea brewing. A small but sturdy woman, she had to stand on tiptoe to kiss the forehead of her son as he handed over the tin of fresh milk. "My beautiful *Marteen*," she said with a sigh.

"Mornin', Mother," he mumbled, removing his cap and returning it to its peg.

His father clomped in, smelling of hay. He stretched and ran his fingers through his thick red hair. "A good day for workin', aye," he grunted. He gave his wife a perfunctory kiss and sat down to eat with his son. The men fell to and smeared home-churned butter on their soda bread, rich with raisins and caraway seeds. They ate noisily, hungrily, stoking their engines for a long morning of work.

About halfway through the meal his mother cleared her throat. "Michael, Teddy's come home," she said in a hushed voice.

Mike Clancy abruptly stopped chewing and looked up. His eyes narrowed. "Come again?" he said.

"Teddy's come home," she repeated evenly. "He arrived last evening and stayed at Mrs. Maloney's inn. I expect that he will come here today."

"And how did you find this out?"

"He sent the message over with the Maloney boy."

Martin's heart was racing. The electricity between his parents was crackling. "Mother," he ventured, "do you mean Uncle Teddy?"

"One and the same," she replied.

"My God, he's been gone since —"

"Since you were a babe and he walked out on the family to seek his fortune in America," sneered his father. "No good bum, that's what he always was, and always will be!"

"Michael! Not in front of Martin," she hissed.

"He's old enough to know about Teddy." Mike Clancy stared into the eyes of his son and pointed a soupspoon his way. "Look here, boy.

Yer uncle, my own brother, agreed to work this farm with me as long as the family owned it."

"Michael!"

"Quiet, woman! He and I promised your grandfather on his deathbed that we would never give up the farm. Never! And what did he do? Got the wanderlust, he did. Slipped out the middle of the night in September 1917. Left a note tellin' us he had to 'follow his dreams' or some such nonsense. Aye, and left me and yer mother to shoulder the burden of runnin' this farm. He killed my mother, you know. Broke her heart, he did. And now, lo and behold, he's come crawling back." His face had gone a deep crimson.

"He's your brother, Michael."

"The hell he is! He disowned us when he ran out on us! I'll not have him set foot in this house!"

And then, something extraordinary happened. Ann Clancy stood up and leaned forward across the table on her knuckles, which Martin noticed had turned white. In a measured tone she said, "I've already invited him. He'll be here for supper. The issue is closed."

Mike Clancy opened his mouth then shut it. This was the first time Martin had ever seen his father lose control of a situation. But for all his bluster, Mike knew better than to cross his beloved Annie. He drew a deep breath, then exhaled. Incredibly, an almost serene look came over his face. "And what time will we be dinin', dear?" he said.

Chapter Two

Cashel

Martin's eyes followed the progress of Uncle Teddy as he made his way up the winding dirt road from town. He had a suitcase slung over his back and carried a valise, too. There was a bounce in his step, though Martin wondered why he was using a walking stick. He also wondered how the elder Clancy was going to greet his baby brother. As Teddy approached, Martin could see he was wearing a suit and tie, and a straw hat as well. Had his uncle become a dandy in America?

Teddy's face brightened as he recognized his nephew at the front gate. "Ah, Martin, you've got so big!" he roared. The two embraced and Teddy pounded his back. "You're a full-grown man, you are!" Teddy was darker and smaller in frame than Mike Clancy was. In fact, he was smaller than his nephew. Martin took his valise and the two of them marched off toward the whitewashed cottage, where Ann stood in the doorway. While beaming and waving at her he said sideways to Martin, "Yer da wants to murder me, I'll bet."

"Yes, Uncle Ted."

"Well, seein' you makes up for any mischief he has in store for me."

As they approached the house, Mike emerged from the stable, wiping his hands. The brothers eyed each other warily, like prizefighters in the opening round.

"Mike," said Teddy with a nod.

"'Lo, Ted," replied Mike.

Ann motioned to Martin to follow her into the house. They left the brothers outside and closed the heavy wooden door. In the ensuing

11

minutes they could hear at different times talking, yelling, crying, and finally, laughing. The brothers entered the cottage, arms slung around each other's shoulders. The Clancys' civil war was over, at least for the time being.

During a special feast of mutton and potatoes, Teddy regaled his family with stories of the United States and a wonderful city called Boston, where he'd lived. It was bigger than Dublin, with trolley cars, automobiles, fancy restaurants and high-class people. Of course, Teddy had only been working in a restaurant, but the pay was steady and life in America was grand. Mike and Ann took Teddy's narrative with a grain of salt, as he was known to exaggerate upon occasion. But Martin was enthralled. He asked question after question, which quite irritated his father. However, Teddy welcomed Martin's inquiries and seemed to relish his role as world traveler.

Finally, Mike stood up and declared the evening officially over. "Heavy work to do tomorrow, we'd better get to sleep."

Martin opened his mouth to protest, but Teddy deftly laid his hand on his nephew's shoulder and piped, "Right you are, Mikey. Time for the sack." The two of them clambered into the loft, where they'd fashioned a makeshift bed for Teddy.

As they sat on the edge of their beds in their long underwear, Martin got up the courage to ask his uncle why he'd come back. "Well now," he said, "as happens many times in life, there was a woman, Martin. A great beauty, and I've always been one to have his head turned by a great beauty. And she was in love with me, y'see. Well, I didn't exactly feel the same way. It got a little complicated, as affairs of the heart sometimes do. I won't go into all the whys and wherefores, but I felt it best to come home."

There was an uncomfortable silence, and Martin felt bad for prying.

"But enough about me, boy. Don't you want to know what I brought you from the States?"

Martin grinned. "Sure I do!" he cried.

"All right, quiet now, or yer da will be after the both of us." He rooted around in the big black suitcase and pulled out a pair of bulky leather gloves and some white balls with colorful red stitching. He tossed one of the gloves to Martin, who slipped it on and examined it curiously.

"Know what this is, Martin?"

"Too big for a work glove," he said, feeling the smooth, oiled leather. "I've no idea."

"It's a baseball glove, son. Ya use it to play the grandest game there ever was. In America, it's the national sport. Thousands go to watch it every day, except the Sabbath, of course." He tossed a baseball underhand to his nephew, who caught it with his bare hand. Teddy chuckled. "That's what the glove's for," he said. "Ya use it to catch the ball. And this, me boy, is a bat." He handed the light brown Louisville Slugger to Martin, which the boy had mistaken earlier for a walking stick. This was no walking stick.

"My God, it's a club!" he marveled.

"Guess what you use it for?" queried Teddy.

"Striking the ball?"

"Ah, now yer catchin' on," he said, smiling broadly. "Look at the quality of the wood, boy. It's a grand weapon, all right. Now, regard the signature on the barrel."

Martin squinted in the flickering candlelight. "George 'Babe' Ruth."

"Aye. The Babe, the Bambino, the Sultan of Swat! An American hero who's larger than life, as well known as the President! And you know why? I'll tell you why. Because he can knock one of these white spheroids here over the fence of any ballpark in the Major Leagues! Oh, if you could see him, Martin. He's a giant of a man, bigger than your father is, even. And he's loved by all, especially children…all because he can play this game of baseball as none other."

Teddy's enthusiasm had thoroughly permeated Martin's body. "Can I learn to play this game?" he said breathlessly.

"Of course ya can. You're strong as an ox, and you're good at sports, aren't you?"

"Yes! I was the best in school at football and hurling!"

"Well then," said Teddy, slapping his thighs, "tomorrow after our chores I will begin to instruct you in the finer points of the game. Sleep well, boy."

But Martin did not sleep well. He lay awake for many hours, clutching the black fielder's glove. When he awoke the next morning, it was still in his grasp.

13

Chapter Three

Cashel

Teddy had arrived at the onset of spring, and there was no shortage of work to be done on the Clancy farm. The men busied themselves with the daily tasks of the season. First, the stone walls that surrounded the vast farm had to be rebuilt. Rainwater ditches had to be repaired and in some cases re-dug. As the ground began to dry out, plowing began. The Clancy men took turns behind Dickens, grunting with every row. Ann was already setting out pieces of potatoes to sprout.

Despite these backbreaking tasks, Martin attacked his work with a fervor that made Mike Clancy take notice. Faster work meant more time before and after dinner for Martin and his uncle to practice the odd game they called baseball. Teddy had even built up a mound of dirt behind the stable and packed it down. He then measured the distance from the stable wall. For some reason, he said, it had to be sixty feet, six inches American. Then, he'd painted a white square on the wooden slats and had Martin throw a ball against it. Every evening as Mike enjoyed his pipe he could hear the wok-wok-wok of the ball smashing the wall. Craziness!

Teddy was forever instructing him with a patience far beyond what his older brother had ever possessed. "Now show me a fastball!" Wok! "Fadeaway!" Wok! Inside corner, outside corner, over-the-top, snap-the-wrist, follow through...words and phrases Mike could not comprehend, nor did he want to. Such foolishness. But as long as it did not affect the boy's work...

*　　*　　*　　*

"Tell me about the Babe again," said Martin. The teen never could get enough of baseball. He was overjoyed when Teddy produced a dog-eared copy of the *Reach Baseball Guide and Rule Book,* and devoured it page by page. Before long, he knew the history of both major leagues and the statistics of all the key players. But the Babe was his favorite. He had even tacked up a picture of Ruth in uniform over his bed, which Ann considered somewhat sacrilegious.

As much as Martin loved to hear about Ruth, Teddy loved to sing his praises. "A good man on the worst of days," was his usual prelude. "The key to the Babe, Martin, what sets him apart, is that he was an accomplished hurler before he became an outfielder. He had a wonderful pitching record until the management of the Red Sox realized they could make more money if he played every day. So now, he hits prodigious home runs and patrols the outfield. Ya would think that Harry Frazee, the right idiot who owned the Sox, would've held onto him, but no. The damn fool sold him to the Yankees, of all teams, and we haven't won a thing in Boston since!"

Martin ascertained that this was a touchy subject with Teddy and changed the topic. "When can I learn to hit, Uncle Ted?"

"I'll tell you what, boy. T'morrah we'll get after it, but it won't be easy at first. You'll have to bat against me, and I've a pretty fair arm."

"I know I can learn. I'm getting better at my pitching, isn't that true?"

"Aye, yer not bad, boy," he said, remembering how frightening it was becoming to step in against his nephew. Martin's fastball was simply explosive, and lately they'd been replacing splintered slats in the stable at an alarming rate.

By May, the bogs were dry enough to cut turf, and the heavy slabs were stacked on the ground to cure. Soon the cabbage, which had been planted in March, had to be cut. The potatoes were turned over in the field and picked as needed.

And Martin batted, for at least an hour each day. He had a bit of a problem with curveballs, but began rocketing Teddy's mediocre fastballs all over the place. It was a good thing that acres of land behind the stable were plowed flat, or they would have lost the balls. As it was, Teddy had

15

to dry them out over the fire every few days and re-sew the stitching on occasion. Rainy days (and there were many of them) were especially infuriating, but it was a rare day they went without practice. An Irishman doesn't give rain a second thought, for it is a blessing.

Mike Clancy began to grumble about his son's dedication to this silly endeavor, but Ann cautioned him to leave his son be. "He'll soon tire of it, dear," she soothed. But there was more to it, of course. It was always Uncle Teddy this and Uncle Teddy that with his son. Maybe the workload was easier now, but Mike began to rue the day his brother had returned.

Summer came to Cashel in all its glory, and the chief task at hand was the harvesting of the hay. Each farmer kept a section of meadowland for hay depending on how many animals he had to feed. Since the Clancys had only Amy and Dickens, the job was not impossible for the three men to handle. Often the men from several farms would join to work as a team in what was called "cooring." This was to both lessen the task and to save time, since the hay must be cut, gathered, and covered up for winter. Mike did not care to join with the community, however, probably because he had so little hay himself. It was typical of his isolationism.

Now Martin was engaged with picking up rolling balls and catching what Teddy called "flies." Like everything else about this damned game, Martin seemed to be making strides rather quickly. Mike Clancy began a slow simmer, wondering how in the world his son could be sustained by a sport which was known to only two men in County Tipperary, if not the whole of Ireland. Good Lord, what was the point?

Autumn crept in and the weather, almost imperceptibly, changed. During October and November, the turnips and potatoes were pulled up and stored in covered pits for winter use. Many trips were made by horse cart to the bog to bring back dried turf for fuel. The animals were put in the stable for protection from the wet days of winter.

In the shadow of the omnipresent castle walls, uncle and nephew continued to refine the skills of the latter, one day concentrating on hitting, one day on pitching, and so forth. The bat that Teddy had brought from America was now chipped and scarred, with tiny nails throughout that mended cracks. The dirty, misshapen balls could hardly

16

be distinguished from field potatoes. Mike, who had never known the joys of sport in his life, ground his teeth. With each crack of the bat a wedge between him and his son was being driven.

Winter came just in time.

In Ireland, winter is so wet and foggy that little outside work could be done. The men might travel the nearest city to find factory work or even go to work in England for a few months. But Mike Clancy would have none of that. He preferred to stay on the farm, repairing tools and caring for the animals. He whiled away the hours patching harnesses or repairing furniture. This did not deaden the gnawing pain of jealousy in his gut, however, and he became generally miserable.

Martin and Teddy were unhappy also, but for a different reason. The weather had severely limited their practices, and sometimes they could only get in one or two a week. Being careful to avoid Mike, they talked baseball at every opportunity, and Martin became a walking encyclopedia of the sport, though he had never witnessed a game. He also began to ask more questions about the United States and its customs. Teddy was only too happy to share his knowledge with his nephew, who had a seemingly insatiable curiosity about baseball and all things American.

Christmas was a disaster for the Clancy family. In Ireland, it is celebrated quietly, simply, with the exchange of gifts being secondary. On Christmas Day 1926, things went well until Teddy pulled from beneath his bed a long box that had arrived via the mail some weeks before. It held a brand-new bat and a half-dozen baseballs. Martin's eyes lit up at the sight of his presents, but Mike Clancy had had enough. With catlike quickness, he grabbed the bat from Martin's hands and snapped it over his knee with a resounding crack, as if it were a twig. Then, in a flash, he had pinned his younger brother to the wall, clutching a fistful of his shirt. Teddy's toes barely touched the floor.

"Mikey, fer God's sake!" pleaded Teddy. "Why are ya doin' this?"

"Don't ya play dumb with me," he growled. "You surprised me, brother. I never thought you had it in ya to commit yourself to anybody or anything in this world, but I was wrong. Ever since ya came crawlin' back here you've been filling the boy's head with fairytales and nonsense, tryin' to turn him against me. Oh, I've been watching you,

17

Teddy, but like always I let it go, because of Annie and because yer me brother and the Bible says to forgive. But I'm warnin' you. You try to come between me and my boy and I'll tear you apart, brother or no."

Martin, appalled, tried to separate the two men, but Mike backhanded him across the face with his huge free paw and sent him reeling to the floor where he sat, fixed with the awesome strength of his father.

Clancy looked down upon his stricken son. "And you," he sneered. "Here I've built this farm to what it is through hard work and sweat, just so you can carry on, as I did for my father. But that's not good enough for you. Starry-eyed dreamer! This is your life! It's time you be a man and accept yer responsibility or I'll, I'll..." He never finished the sentence, letting go of Teddy and stalking out of the house with a crash that left the heavy wooden door shaking on its hinges.

Ann, who had never moved from her seat at the table, smoothed her apron and stared into her lap. "Mother of God, now you've done it, Teddy Clancy," she said. "Yer brother's a good man. Many don't understand him, but he is a decent man, a caring man. However, he cannot comprehend the affection the two of you are lavishing upon yer games. I'll have to ask, for the sake of this household, that you refrain from practicing yer base-ball from now on."

"But Mother—" spluttered Martin.

"There will be no backtalk, young man! I have defended you many a time when your father was cross with you, but even I can see how this fancy of yours has overwhelmed you. Yer not the same Martin! And you, Teddy Clancy. You should be ashamed of yerself for leadin' the lad astray. When are ye going to grow up? Ya can't play at games forever.

"Now, I've said my piece, but mark my words. There will be no more base-ball, and no further discussion of the subject!" With that, she arose and busied herself by the fire.

From his seat in the corner, Martin could see his mother's eyes brimming with tears. He took the splintered bat and committed it to the flames.

*   *   *   *

That night the two men lay awake in the loft, staring into the

18

blackness. Teddy was wondering just what he had done that was so awful when Martin whispered, "Uncle Ted, I want to go to America."

Teddy turned to face his nephew's bed. "Nah, boy, ya don't mean that. Yer just upset that you've angered yer parents."

"No, sir, that's not it a'tall. It's just that…I want a chance to do something special, to be somebody. I'm very frightened that I'm going to live my whole life on this godforsaken farm without ever accomplishing something I can be proud of. At least you had the chance to pursue your dreams. But what about me?" He choked back a sob. "I'm almost eighteen years old now, but to them I'm still a child. I'll always be me father's son, that's all. Don't ya think I deserve more than that in life? Didn't you once feel the same way?"

"Aye, boy."

Martin slipped from his bed, and now Teddy Clancy could feel his nephew's breath on his face as he knelt before him in the dark. "Please, Uncle Ted. You know people in Boston. You could arrange an audition for me with the Red Sox—"

"Now wait just a min—"

"I'm begging you, Uncle Ted. Please get me out of here." He buried his face in Teddy's quilt and wept.

Teddy was torn. On the one hand, he was cursing himself for bringing this all about and playing the bigshot with his nephew. On the other hand, there was a chance, although it was the longest of long shots…

He stroked Martin's curls and whispered, "Shush now, stop yer cryin', boy. I'll help you. There'll be the devil ta pay before we're through, but I'll not desert you now. Just give me some time ta think, all right?"

Snuffling, Martin hugged his uncle. "Thank you, sir, thank you," he rasped.

For the first time in his life, Teddy Clancy realized, he was absolutely, irreversibly committed.

Chapter Four

The North Atlantic - March, 1927

Martin clung to the railing of the passenger ship *Royal Grenadier* and looked out over the gray ocean. The sea rose and fell in menacing swells, but he did not take ill, as many others on board had. In fact, he was relieved to be out on the promenade deck. He'd grown tired of lying on the bed in his tiny third class cabin, bouncing a baseball off the steel door and catching it. He knew he was only one day away from Boston now. As he peered from beneath his snap-brimmed cap, he reflected on the complicated chain of events that had led him to this point.

Uncle Ted, true to his word, had made contact with Monsignor Patrick Garvey, an old friend of his in Boston. Msgr. Garvey had taken a shine to Teddy upon his arrival in 1917, and Teddy had become deeply involved in church affairs. Garvey's parish, which was mostly first-generation Irish Catholic, was among the largest in Boston, and Teddy played a major role in holiday celebrations, fundraising, and the like. It was Garvey who had arranged for Teddy's secret passage back to Ireland. Garvey pulled it off without anyone's knowledge, including one Molly O'Herlihy, who had been dogging him for the better part of a month. Teddy was no different from many Irish men who traditionally marry late, but Molly was so smitten with the sweet talking Teddy that she had become borderline psychotic over him. This genuinely scared him, as did Molly's brutish longshoremen brothers, who had been linked to various violent crimes on the docks and were feared even by their friends. Not only did Teddy want to stay unmarried, he wanted to stay alive and unmarried. If only he hadn't slept with her!

20

Teddy, unfortunately, had recognized his dilemma far too late. Molly, who considered herself betrothed, came after him with a vengeance, even going so far as to interrupt Garvey's homily during a Sunday high mass to loudly inquire as to his whereabouts. She had clearly gone off the deep end, and the monsignor felt he was doing Teddy a huge favor by smuggling him out of Boston on a tramp steamer bound for Cork. It was not without sadness that Garvey gave up his right hand man, but a true fear for Teddy's safety overrode any feelings of distaste for his somewhat unchivalrous behavior. Indeed, Garvey knew that the O'Herlihy boys made no allowance for men of the cloth when it came to exacting their punishments.

Anyway, Garvey had promised that, should Teddy ever return to the States, he would do all he could for him. This led to their correspondence during the winter of 1926, which in turn induced Garvey's promise to not only help Martin get settled should he come over, but to wangle a tryout for him at Fenway Park. The good monsignor, as it happened, was also a rabid Red Sox fan, tracing his loyalty back to the days of the Royal Rooters, a band of fanatics who had attended Sox games in the late 1800s for the express purpose of distracting their opponents with continuous chants and singing, especially the song "Tessie." It also happened that two of Garvey's most esteemed parishioners were a pair of fine boys of the Auld Sod: Bob Quinn, the current owner and general manager, and Bill "Rough" Carrigan, the field manager. Yes, markers of all kinds were being called in, and Martin was to be the chief benefactor of these machinations.

The plan had been set in motion on the night of March 13. A motor car picked up Martin in town and proceeded to Cahir, from which point he boarded a train to the industrial port of Cork. Then he made the transfer to the *Royal Grenadier*, barely making the last boarding call. Teddy had booked passage for him with the remainder of his life savings.

Leaving his house had been the hardest part, of course. Martin had secretly packed all of his worldly belongings, including his glove and some baseballs, in Teddy's suitcase. They had waited until midnight, when Mike and Ann were surely asleep, and then crept like thieves down the ladder. Teddy pushed Martin toward the door, but he balked. "I've got to look upon them," he whispered.

Teddy rolled his eyes. "All right, but be quick about it, we're on a tight schedule."

Martin parted the curtains and squinted through the gloom. Both Mike Clancy and his wife lay on their back, enjoying the blissful sleep of the weary. He blinked back salty tears as he realized that he might well never see these people again. The boy crossed himself, backed out of the alcove and closed the curtains. He emerged from the cottage door somewhat composed, but then came face-to-face with the Rock of Cashel, in dark contrast against the moon. It towered above him like a sentinel, damning him. He fairly shook in Teddy's too-small shoes. Just once more, he wanted to climb the great hill and sit in the drafty sanctuary of Cormac's Chapel in the cathedral. It was his secret hiding place, remarkable for its 12th century wall carvings and ornamentation, beloved to Martin for its peace and quiet. Had not Teddy shaken him by the shoulders, he might have stayed rooted to the spot till dawn.

"Let's go, boy. There's no time fer lollygaggin', now! You know what you have to do, and so forth?"

"Yes, sir."

"And you have all yer papers and pocket money?"

"Yes, sir, I checked."

"Then yer off, now."

The two men faced each other. Martin extended his hand. "Thank you, Uncle Ted. I know you've sacrificed a lot for me."

"Ah, boy, 'tisn't much, considering I got you involved in all this in the first place. Just do me a favor and be a smashing success, because then maybe, just maybe, yer da will then talk to me again someday."

"I'll make you proud of me, I promise."

"All right now, let go of me hand and be on your way, and whatever you do, don't look back, not once!"

They broke, and Martin tramped off into the mist.

Chapter Five

Cashel

Dear Mike,

By the time you read this note you will be angry at Martin, and you will probably hate me altogether, but hear me out.

The boy wants his own life, that is for true. He has gone out on his own to try to make a name for himself. He wants you to be proud of him, but he feels that he will never be one for the farming life. I cannot tell you where he has gone because I would not put it past you to drag him back to Cashel by the scruff of his neck. But I swear to you that he will be looked after. You do not have to believe me but you will sleep better if you do.

As for myself, well you would not expect me to hang about for the beating I would surely be dealt due to the boy's departure. Therefore, I have decided to venture north to sort out my life and hopefully make my fortune. More than that, I cannot tell you because I do not know myself. Do not forsake me, brother. Someday I will make it up to you. Until then I remain,
Your loving brother
Ted

The younger Clancy looked over his work in the gloom of the cottage, words that had been written days before in anticipation of his escape. He set it down on the table, wondering if he would ever stop running away from his problems. But there was no way he could survive on the farm any longer, especially under the malevolent stare of his brother. Forget the thrashing he'd receive; the alienation would be far worse.

He slipped outside to the barn where his packed grip lay hidden under some loose hay. There was no time for sentimentality. He had to get going quickly. At a brisk trot he cleared the front gate and headed northeast in the general direction of Dublin. There he would look up a crony from his Boston days, one Brendan Cudahy, a tough who like himself had been forced to leave the States under dubious circumstances and whose family owned a pub on Aston Quay in the city's center. Whether or not Brendan would be there was anybody's guess; he was changeable as the sky. However, he did present a ray of hope. So, fingering the lone ten-pound note in his pocket, Teddy set forth towards his future.

Time passed slowly as he trooped through the early morning fog, occasionally switching the grip from one hand to another. He munched on a piece of soda bread he'd nicked from the pantry, saving a lump of cheddar for later on. He paused at a cold stream to drink and freshen up. After gulping down a few mouthfuls of the sweetly frigid water, he ran some through his curly black hair. Then he sat back against a tree to towel off and ponder his situation.

By now Mike would be raising holy hell; he felt sorry for Ann. Working the farm by himself would be damn near impossible, and he couldn't afford to hire help. Perhaps Ted could ease the burden by sending him some money once he had established himself. Pushing the guilt from his mind, Teddy admired the clouds that were starting to break up, allowing thin shafts of sunlight here and there. He hoped the weather would be with him for the journey, for unlike his brother he'd become a city boy not used to dealing with the elements. Even now, he felt uncomfortable in his damp Wellies, caked and muddy from the morning's travels.

Suddenly from around a bend in the road came a braying sound, followed by some rich Gaelic cursing. A vegetable-laden wagon appeared, pulled by a donkey and driven by an old, shriveled octogenarian with pipe in mouth and cap pulled down low. Teddy gathered his meager belongings and sidled up to the creeping wagon. "Mornin', sir," he said with his most winning smile.

"Mornin', me boy," replied the old man from the corner of his mouth. "A bit early to be out in the middle of nowhere, it is."

"And isn't that the fact," agreed Teddy, "and if t'were not for my misfortune last night I'd be well along and not here."

"Misfortune, you say." The man's voice was not questioning in the least.

Lord, thought Teddy, *what a sourpuss*.

"Aye," he pressed on, "it's me horse. Mind you, 'e's not a beauty, just a plow horse he is, but last night I tied him to yonder tree whilst I slept an' 'e's run off, leaving me to fend for myself. Now it seems I'll never complete me journey. I'll never see me gram again."

The old man reined in the donkey and looked down at him. "I don't follow."

Teddy had to fight from grinning. Instead, he hung his head and drooped his shoulders with a sigh. "It's me gramma, she's not long for this world; I got the news two days ago. And I swore if it was the last thing I'd do, I'd see her face before she departed this earth." A tear worked its way down his cheek.

"Where ya from, lad?" asked the old man.

"Cahir, sir," he said, raising his head and wiping his eyes. "Name's Sean… Sean Burke. Please excuse me bawlin'."

"No need for apologies," the man grumbled. "I'm goin' as far as Kilkenny, to the market. Would ya like to come aboard?"

"Sure and 'tis I'm blessed!" cried Teddy, vaulting into the seat beside the startled old man. "Kilkenny's exactly where I'm headed. I'll see me gram yet!"

After twenty or so bumpy miles, the historic town of Kilkenny came into view. Teddy was quite thankful, for despite the fact that he had not had to walk this distance, the old man was terrible company, and his arse hurt from the wooden wagon wheels passing over the countless ruts and rocks along the way. He bid the old man farewell at the market, pinched a couple of his potatoes from the back of the wagon, and went on his way to explore. Kilkenny was very interesting. Although a relatively small town, its winding streets that rose and plunged seemed quite medieval. Of course, if he'd wanted history he'd have never left Cashel. No, Kilkenny was definitely not the kind of place for Teddy Clancy.

After the fast life of Boston, only Dublin could hope to compare in his mind. But what would present day Dublin be like? The last time he'd been there was 1917, the year after the Easter Rising. The Brits had put down the rebellion, of course, and parts of the city lay in ruins as a result. It was just one of the many factors in his decision to leave for the United States. Ireland seemed dead, or at least dying. He'd wanted adventure, a clean slate. And he'd gotten it, in spades. The States were created, it seemed, for people like him, people who with a little pluck and luck could make a name for themselves and live the good life. Through his night job as a maître d' in one of the swank restaurants in Boston and his affiliation with Monsignor Garvey, Teddy had rubbed elbows with the wealthy and the influential. He'd hated, absolutely hated, to return, and it was only the time spent with his nephew that had kept him sane. Maybe someday he would gather the wherewithal to return, but he'd never accomplish that on the farm. Dublin was the key, his only hope. Somehow, he would hit it big there. Apply a little American know-how and make a killing. But at what? He had no clue.

Teddy stopped into a pub, sipped a pint of Guinness, and helped himself to a hard-boiled egg. The licorice-hued brew went down oh so smoothly, and he nursed his drink for a good half hour. Then he availed himself to the washroom and was on his way. Deeming it unwise to spend some of his remaining money on lodging, he found for himself on the outskirts of town a deserted though not crumbled round tower, one of the hundreds that dotted the landscape of Ireland. The inside of the tower had a diameter of only fifteen feet or so, but the tower itself rose some seventy feet, with a winding stone staircase built into the wall and leading to a single window near the top. No doubt, the local inhabitants had used this in the days of Viking attacks as a belfry and watchtower. Positioned on a hillock, Teddy had a commanding view of the countryside in all directions. He stood there for some time, propped in the opening on his elbows like some medieval sentinel, watching for nothing in particular.

Evening was coming, and the hills took on a bluish hue. White mists hung in the hollows and the only movement discernible was the rushing current of a nearby brook. He returned to the floor of the tower, cleared an area, and made a fire, burying his stolen potatoes deep in the embers.

He pulled from his jacket a flask of whiskey and watched the smoke spiral upwards into the blackness.

The next morning, he woke with a start, temporarily disoriented. The fire he'd built had long since gone out. Teddy found himself covered with dew and chilled to the bone. He took a pull from his flask, shivered, and ventured out into the sunlight. He judged the time to be around 7:30 AM and cursed himself for oversleeping. "Time to get cracking, laddie," he said to himself. Within minutes, he was off again.

Along winding roads, he passed whitewashed farmhouses and ruined castles, churches in various states of disrepair, herds of sheep, rolling hills crisscrossed with stone walls and streams. There was the omnipresent mixture of greens and browns. Stacks of dark, cut peat lined sections of the road like huge chocolate squares for the gods. The smoke of turf fires hung in the air. A beautiful day, all things considered. He was twice lucky to meet people who let him sit in the back of their wagons for a while. The second one, a fair, freckled lass with blue eyes, was momentarily startled when he lapsed to the American vernacular and asked her for a "ride," forgetting that back over here the phrase had quite another meaning. But Teddy's smile and a quick apology eased her ire, and he dozed on a bed of cabbages for an hour or two as they bumped along.

She let him off at her family's house, greeting her father, who leaned on the lower portion of the house's half-door and smoked his pipe. Over the man's shoulder, Teddy could see an orange fire burning and smelled what seemed to be rabbit stew, but the man's stern visage implied that he'd best be moving along. However, the girl, whose name was Molly (which had brought a shiver) did give him a generous slice of brown bread. "Good day to you, *a colleen*," he'd said with a wink, and was on his way.

Dunlavin, the next town on the road to Dublin, was not reached until well after nightfall. Exhausted, he crept into the Roman Catholic Church and slept sitting up in one of the back pews, comforted in knowing that the next stop would be his destination. He awakened, sore and stiff, to the clang of church bells. Hoping he had not been discovered, Teddy ashamedly dropped a few coins into the collection box and departed. A check of his finances revealed only eight pounds remaining. But enough was enough. "The hell with it," he said, and he strode across the village square to the train station. Luckily, the small ticket office was open. "When's the next train to Dublin?" he inquired.

The clerk behind the counter checked his pocket watch. "Ah, forty minutes, give or take," was the reply.

"Fine. I'll have a single, please." He purchased his ticket and went next door to a bakery, where he purchased some sweet rolls. With some time to kill, he strolled around town a bit, had a cup of tea in the station, and awaited his train. It was almost a half hour late, which was strange for Irish trains, but nothing could dampen his spirits. He stretched out in the nearly deserted passenger car and was lulled to sleep by the clickety-clack of the steel wheels. It was just after noon when Teddy Clancy stepped onto the platform at Pearse Station, refreshed and ready to take on the world.

Chapter Six

Boston

Martin Clancy approached the shores of the United States as the country, under the guidance of president "Silent Cal" Coolidge, was enjoying a period of enormous economic prosperity. Corporations were making large profits and the stock market was taking off, while Prohibition had spawned an explosion in the illegal production and distribution of liquor. Organized crime became a force to be reckoned with. The residual danger—especially in the larger cities—only added to the sizzle. There was also a loosening of social mores, led by women obtaining the right to vote and adopting the carefree lifestyle of the "Jazz Age."

For entertainment, people turned to moving pictures or, on a more personal level, the radio. Through these genres, as well as the flowery printed words of sports writers, athletes in this "Golden Age of Sports" were worshiped as gods. Whether it was Jack Dempsey slugging his way to the heavyweight title, Walter Hagan and Bobby Jones in golf, or the "Galloping Ghost," Red Grange of the gridiron, Americans were looking for heroes. Thus, a character like George Herman Ruth, who overcame a misspent youth and subsequent sequestering in a strict reform school, could rise to a level of prominence unprecedented in American athletic lore, even earning more in salary than the president of the nation. Indeed, in the "Roaring 20s" anything was possible, and no one felt the allure of its siren song more than the young Irishman from Cashel.

It was advantageous that Teddy Clancy had cultivated a benefactor such as Monsignor Patrick Garvey in Boston. As a high-ranking clergyman in a predominately Irish Catholic city, Garvey had been able to procure the necessary papers for Martin, which would sidestep the customary red tape encountered by immigrants of the period coming over from Europe. In effect, he'd been smuggled into the country, though he was blissfully unaware of the illegalities of his crossing. All he knew was that Uncle Teddy's close friend would be there to greet him upon his arrival in Boston, and that was enough for him. The fact that he had celebrated his 18th birthday alone in a cold, damp stateroom aboard the *Royal Grenadier* seemed a small price to pay for the gift he'd been given.

Monsignor Garvey met Martin at the dock with a hearty embrace and a "Welcome to the New World, lad!" He was a big, beefy man with a shock of white hair and a bulbous red nose. Martin could detect the faint smell of whiskey on his breath. "So you've come from the Auld Sod to be a ballplayer, eh? Well, that's a new one. Let's hop in my flivver and get back to St. Catherine's."

The ride to the church rectory was a harrowing experience. Model Ts and trolleys seemed to be flying in all directions. Martin was awed at the tall buildings. And all the different kinds of people! Italians, blacks, Orientals…what a mishmash! It was all too much to sort out at once.

"Would you like to see Fenway, Martin?" asked Garvey, a twinkle in his eye.

"I dearly would, your Eminence!"

"Then look to your left, and cut out the 'Eminence' stuff." They turned the corner of Lansdowne Street and there it was, a redbrick structure as long as a city block.

Construction on Fenway Park had begun in 1911, the ballpark taking its name from the site on which it would rest, a marshy area known as the Fens. It had opened the same week the Titanic had sunk in 1912. The park featured a single-decked grandstand behind home plate, a large wooden bleacher section between the grandstand and the left field corner, wooden bleachers in center, and a wooden pavilion in the right field corner.

With the opening of the park, the fortunes of the club improved, led by outfielder Tris Speaker and pitcher Smoky Joe Wood. They would defeat John McGraw's New York Giants that year in a dramatic World

Series during the park's maiden season. The Sox would repeat as world champions in 1913, 1915, and 1918, now led by their outstanding young pitcher, Babe Ruth, who was also showing a flair for power hitting. However, as the fortunes of the club began to turn after the sale of Ruth to the Yankees in 1920, attendance dropped off; by the time of Clancy's arrival, they were averaging less than 4000 fans per game. But all of this meant little to the young Irishman who was struck dumb by the edifice, and Garvey found it curious that a boy who had lived in the shadow of one of the most romantic castles in all of Europe should be awed by a baseball stadium.

"It's...beautiful," managed Martin.

"And the inside's better, me lad. You'll get yer first look a week from today, when the Sox come north from spring training. It's all been arranged."

"I think I'll die from the wait, your Em—uh, Monsignor."

Garvey smiled. "No need to worry, lad. I've got a few chores that'll keep you busy 'til then."

He was not joking. Martin, in exchange for his room and meals, spent the next seven days cleaning St. Catherine's Church from top to bottom. In a sense, though, he was thankful for a way to work off his nervous energy. He polished every wooden pew, shined every gold fixture, and mopped every floor tile. During his breaks, he walked around Boston in ever-widening circles, and each day he learned something new. Martin especially loved to hear the different languages of the immigrants of the city. He hoped to someday learn them all! And every evening between dinner and prayers he threw against the back wall of the brick rectory, sweating despite the chill, sharpening his deliveries for the big moment.

Finally, it was Monday, April 10. Garvey and the young pitcher climbed into the official parish motorcar of St. Catherine's Church and negotiated the maze of one-way streets that led to Fenway. Then they were there. Garvey turned off the ignition and the engine wheezed, coughed and died. "Time fer another fundraising drive," he muttered.

"Hello, Monsignor!" sang the guard at the *Players Only* entrance.

"Mornin', Bobby!" answered the clergyman. Martin was impressed; Garvey seemed to know everybody. They walked beneath the stands and through a tunnel, emerging in the stands immediately above home plate. After a year of looking at grainy black and white photos, Martin saw his first real baseball diamond. Its color and symmetry, its sheer beauty, made his knees rubbery. He was in love. There was no way for him, then, to know that he was in fact standing in the graveyard of the Majors.

The Boston franchise of the American League was a horror show in flannel during the 1920s. Their precipitous slide from glory had begun on December 26, 1919, when the financially strapped Harry Frazee sold his star pitcher/slugger Babe Ruth to the New York Yankees in order to raise funds for his theatrical endeavors. The Sox were then systematically dismantled as Frazee's attempts to bring a winner to Broadway flopped. Ruth, the cornerstone of the great Yankee dynasty of the 1920s, was followed out of Beantown by such luminaries as Carl Mays, Waite Hoyt, Bullet Joe Bush, Jumpin' Joe Dugan, and a host of others. Yankee owner Jacob Ruppert gleefully picked Frazee's pocket while the Red Sox became trapped in the throes of a decade-long slump. In July of 1923, Frazee could no longer auction his good players, having sold them all, so he sold the team. J.A. "Bob" Quinn, former vice president and general manager of the St. Louis Browns, organized a syndicate that purchased the Sox, making himself president and general manager.

Quinn's ordeal had begun. After he took over the Sox, they finished last in 1923, 1924, 1925 and 1926. Although spirits were high on the day Martin Clancy entered Fenway for the first time, the sportswriters had picked the team for the cellar again. But the anticipation of opening day could bring irrational hope to even the lousiest team and their fans, and both Quinn and his field manager, Bill "Rough" Carrigan, greeted Garvey with a bonhomie that would probably be worn away in a few weeks' time.

"So this is our Irish cousin," laughed Quinn. "Pleased to meet you, son."

Martin eagerly shook hands with the stocky owner and the much larger Carrigan. "I'm pleased to make the acquaintance of you both, sir!" he replied, beaming.

Carrigan, a bear of a man, spread his legs and stuck his hands in the back pockets of his knickers. "Now let me get this straight, son," he growled. "You've never pitched in an organized game of baseball?"

"No sir, but I've practiced all parts of the game, I truly have!"

"I don't doubt that. But there's a huge difference between practice and a real-life game situation. You must realize that."

"I'm willing to do anything it takes to learn, sir," he pleaded.

Quinn cut in. "Bill, why don't we let Martin get a uniform and spikes from Bits and we'll let him throw a little. You know the way downstairs, Monsignor. Why don't you bring him down to the clubhouse?"

"Come, lad," said Garvey, and the two hopefuls hurried off.

Carrigan shook his head. "Mr. Quinn—"

"Don't tell me, Bill, I know. This is crazy. But whoinhell knows? Maybe he'll bring us the luck of the Irish."

"Bob, *we* can't even bring ourselves the luck of the Irish!"

The two men roared.

*   *   *   *

Martin, glove in hand, and his patron wove their way through the Red Sox clubhouse that, despite it being early in the season, already smelled of sweat and liniment. The players, who were dressing for the year's first workout at their stadium, paid no attention to them, other than a few veterans who waved to Garvey. The truth was that the roster had been turning over so quickly from year to year the clergyman recognized few faces.

Bits, the equipment manager, clubhouse man and trainer, quickly sized up Martin and gave him a heavy gray and red road uniform, leggings, ballcap and spikes. Martin went to the far end of the room, away from the occupied lockers, and pulled on the flannels over his long underwear. He felt comfortable in the conventionally baggy shirt and knickers, but the spikes were tight. Having never worn baseball shoes before, it was necessary for Garvey to offer a steadying hand so he could tiptoe across the concrete floor and into the damp, drippy tunnel that led to the dugout.

A few veterans snickered at the sight. "Busher," they muttered.

The young pitcher walked up the steps of the dugout and onto the field. The early spring turf was barely pliable, but his metal cleats dug in, and he rather liked the feeling. He strode toward the backstop, where Carrigan and a catcher, wearing only a mask, waited. Quinn had retired to the stands with Garvey to watch.

"I'm ready, Mr. Carrigan," said Martin.

"All right, son. This is your catcher, Mr. Grover Hartley. I want you to warm up. When you're ready, he'll call the pitches: one finger for a fastball, two for a curve."

"What about my 'fadeaway'?"

"Christ, the kid thinks he's Christy Mathewson," moaned Hartley under his breath.

"Er, that'll be three fingers, son."

Hartley, the Sox' number one catcher and oldest player, turned and jogged to his position behind home plate. He grunted, squatted, and tapped his mitt.

Martin stood atop the mound, swinging his arm to get it loose. His gaze traveled around the entire ballpark, pausing on the disconcerting sight of the left field grandstand, which had burned down the year before and still lay in ruins, a testament to Quinn's precarious financial situation.

"Hey kid, you can buy a postcard later. Start warmin' up!" Hartley was getting tired of catching every Tom, Dick and Harry who came in for a tryout, and he was grumpy.

The young right-hander began soft tossing, then slowly picked up his velocity. After ten pitches, he announced that he was ready. Hartley put down one finger. Martin gave the double windmill windup that his uncle had taught him and drove toward the plate. He grunted in his violent follow-through. The ball rocketed into Hartley's mitt with a *ssschup* that made him smile. He nodded and snapped the ball back to Martin. Once again, the catcher put down the number one. Again, the ball came in, this time with a little hop on it. "Good movement," he said sideways to Carrigan. His hand was stinging beneath the catcher's mitt.

"I can see that," said the manager. "Ask for the curve."

Hartley put down the deuce and Martin pumped and kicked. The ball broke sharply down as it crossed the plate. Hartley turned and glanced at Carrigan, who looked on impassively, his arms folded across his chest.

The other Red Sox were straggling out into the daylight as Martin kept throwing fastballs and curveballs that rarely missed their mark. "Wally Shaner!" bellowed Carrigan. "Grab a bat and step in here!" The outfielder picked out lumber from the row of bats laid out before the dugout, whistling a tune under his breath. He ground his feet into the dirt around home plate. "Does the kid got anything, Grove?" he asked.

"Just stay loose, Wally," cautioned Hartley. He signaled for a curveball.

Whoosh! Shaner's swing at the darting pitch was at best feeble.

"Missed it by a mile, Wally," giggled the catcher.

"That damn thing dropped the foot!" marveled Shaner. "Have a heart, Grover; don't make me look bad in front of the skipper."

"All right. Fastball coming. Get ready." He signaled; Martin nodded, kicked and dealt. Shaner took a tremendous rip but the ball was already in Hartley's mitt. "Just a tad late, Wally boy," he teased.

· For five minutes, Shaner battled the novice, but the most he could manage were a few weak grounders. A crowd started to gather near first base. Slim Harriss, the acknowledged ace of the staff, asked, "Who's the busher?"

"Some mick just off the boat," someone answered.

"Well, don't laugh," said Harriss, "this mick kid ain't bad."

Then, third baseman Billy Rogell stepped in against Martin, but there was little difference in the results. Hartley called for a couple of 'fadeaways' and Rogell nearly threw his back out reaching for them. The cluster of onlookers conversed in muted tones, nodding their heads.

"That's enough," grunted Carrigan. "Clancy, grab a bat and go hit. Charlie Ruffing, why don't you throw?"

Martin shrugged his shoulders and jogged from the mound. He picked up the closest bat and made his way to the plate. The bat had a light feel to it; he was not aware that the Ruth model he'd been using back home was the weightiest made. He tapped the club, which was stained with tobacco juice and licorice, on the plate, then cocked it behind his head. Nodding that he was ready, he faced the future Hall of Famer.

Ruffing fed him an assortment of fastballs, curves and changeups, and Martin represented himself well. He drove a few Ruffing pitches all the way to Duffy's Cliff, a ten-foot embankment in front of the left-field wall. Named after former Sox leftfielder Duffy Lewis, who had played the hill masterfully, it posed a threat to those who chased fly balls. Therefore, the fielders merely let Martin's blasts roll up the cliff to the wall, which would one day be transfigured into the Green Monster.

Clancy's tryout lasted all of fifteen minutes, but it was enough for Messrs. Quinn and Carrigan. As Martin toweled off in the deserted clubhouse, the owner put a fatherly hand on his shoulder. "Son, you did well out there today, and we're impressed."

"Thank you, Mr. Quinn!" he gushed.

"Don't thank me yet. As I was saying, you did well, and Carrigan likes you. But you have no game experience. We've got to send you out."

Martin panicked. "No sir, ya can't do that, ya can't send me home—"

"No, no," Carrigan said soothingly. "What I mean is that we are going to send you to a minor-league club to get some seasoning, pitching in real games. Then, if you show progress, who knows? You may end up back here with us before too long."

Martin was relieved. "Where will you be sendin' me then, sir?"

Quinn frowned. The Red Sox, who operated on a shoestring, had virtually no farm system. "Well, we have a working agreement with Wilkes-Barre in the New York-Penn league, kind of. I'm friends with the manager, Mike Connick, and I'm sure he'll take you on. He's one of *us*, you know." He shot the youngster a wink. "Let me square it with him today. You be here tomorrow with your things and we'll get you on a train down there."

The young pitcher's heart was bursting with joy. "I'll be here bright and early, Mr. Quinn. And don't you worry; I'll be back before you know it."

Quinn patted him on the head and walked from the room. *I wonder if this happens with the Yankees?* he mused. Probably not. But, if by some chance the kid did make it, Quinn would be hailed in Boston as a genius for finding a hero—an *Irish* hero—for his success-starved fans. He left the ballpark with the sound of clicking turnstiles in his head.

Chapter Seven

Dublin, Ireland

Teddy approached a member of the *Garda Siochana*, or local police, who was positioned outside the train station. A roly-poly man with red cheeks, he cheerfully gave Clancy directions to Aston Quay. Teddy thanked him and moved along, past red brick Georgian mansions with fine doors, fan lights and little iron balconies. Vestiges of old Dublin.

The crowds he passed through were different from those of Boston. There seemed to be more laughter, and the pace was decidedly slower. He did notice that the British red that had adorned pillar-boxes and mail vans had been replaced with green. The names of the streets were now in Gaelic. In contrast to this burst of national pride was the disturbing increase of beggars, especially children. Here and there, a building bore the pockmarks of the violence of the past decade. Teddy approached Aston Quay just as a heavy rain began to fall. He scanned the dirty brown River Liffey as it churned beneath O'Connell Bridge. It reminded him somewhat of the Charles in Boston, but more threatening.

Had Teddy not been searching for it he surely would have missed Cudahy's Pub, which was wedged between two nondescript storefronts facing the Liffey. It was hard to decide if the front window was stained glass or just plain dirty. He took a deep breath and entered the smoky establishment, nearly tripping over a prone figure on the floor before him.

"Get out!" a male voice thundered. "Stick yer bloody hands in me till, will you? Get out of here and never come back! I swear if I see you again I'll kill you!"

Teddy flattened himself against the wall as a blur sped towards him, snatched up the fallen man by his shirt collar and trouser belt, and hurled him out onto the sidewalk. Then the attacker paused and turned slowly, the grimace on his face melting to a broken-toothed smile as recognition seized his brain. "Teddy? Teddy Clancy?"

"As ever was," whispered the still-frightened visitor.

"TEDDY CLANCY!" he screamed. Hugging him tightly, the man lifted Clancy a foot off the ground, swung him around and set him down with a bang Teddy felt from his heels to his shoulders. "God save the good work, it's me old mate from Beantown! And what the devil are ye doing back here?"

"Come to see you, pally," he answered, regaining his composure.

Brendan Cudahy ushered him across the floor, elbowing patrons out of the way. Although a tad smaller than Teddy's brother, Brendan was incredibly strong, barrel chested and hulky. Wild reddish-brown hair and a thick mustache added to his fiery demeanor. Depositing Teddy roughly on a bar stool, he quickly drew a pint for his shaky visitor. Teddy had gulped nearly half the Guinness before he realized he had no reason to be afraid. In a flash Cudahy changed from Neanderthal to charming host. "*Slainte*," he began, raising his glass, and Teddy returned the salute. "Christ, but you're the sight for sore eyes," he said, wiping foam from his mustache. "Now what in the world brings you to this fine alehouse? I thought you was in Boston."

"I was. Got back some months ago." He licked some foam from his upper lip.

"How come? I thought you were in yer element there, runnin' that posh eatery of yours."

"I was," he said wistfully. "I had a bad situation."

"Money?"

"Worse."

"Woman?"

"Uh-huh."

"Irish?"

"Aye."

"And Catholic?"

"As the Pope in Rome."

"Say no more. But ya should've known better, boyo." He drew each of them another pint.

"Well, ya live and ya learn, they say. But what about yourself? One day you were there, and the next day, poof! There were all kinds of crazy rumors flyin' around as to your whereabouts. Some people even maintained you were dead. It wasn't till 1920 I heard for sure that you were back 'ere. What happened? And why didn't you let me know? I thought we were pals, Brendan."

Cudahy rubbed his eyes, ran his hand through his hair, and scratched the back of his neck. He seemed to be debating within himself as to whether or not he should open up. Maybe the Guinness had loosened him up, because he leaned across the bar, dropping an elbow into a puddle of stout. "Okay, I'll tell ya, Ted Clancy, but only because I trust you. I still remember the time I owed that wop Colletti some dough, he sent a couple of his thugs out for me, and you hid me until I could get up the jack. I know you wouldn't say nothin'."

"Of course not!" rasped Teddy, somewhat hurt.

"All right then, listen sharp. Does the 1919 World Series ring a bell?"

Teddy's breath caught in his throat. Everyone in America had heard of the 1919 Series, and what would become famous as the Black Sox Scandal. The contest had pitted the powerful American League champion Chicago White Sox against the Cincinnati Reds of the National League in a best-of-nine format, partly to increase the popularity of the sport, and partly to generate more revenue.

The White Sox, who were loaded with talent from top to bottom, most notably the legendary outfielder Shoeless Joe Jackson, future Hall of Fame second baseman Eddie Collins, and knuckleball pitcher Eddie Cicotte, had been established as heavy favorites in the Series under the guidance of first year manager Kid Gleason. The Pale Hose had taken the AL pennant by 3½ games over the formidable Cleveland Indians. When compared on paper to the upstart Reds, it appeared to be no contest.

But things were not copacetic in the White Sox locker room. Tension had arisen between the players and their penurious owner, Charles Comiskey, over issues ranging from promised-but-unpaid player performance bonuses to unlaundered uniforms.

Thus, when the Cincinnati ballclub took the Series in eight games, eyebrows were raised and investigations launched. Although the sordid details would not fully come to light for another year, the result would be the lifetime banishment of eight "Black Sox" players, including Jackson and Cicotte; the establishment of a supreme Commissioner of Baseball to monitor the integrity of the game henceforth; and the near destruction of the sport because of its infiltration by gamblers. Thankfully, a savior had arrived to restore baseball as the National Pastime: George Herman Ruth. But the memory of the Black Sox incident still seemed fresh.

"Sure and I remember," Teddy said. "It made the front pages for weeks. Eight of 'em got tossed outta baseball for throwin' the Series, Joe Jackson and that crew. What of it?"

"I was in on it, is what of it."

Teddy squinted at Cudahy. "Come now, Brendan. You had connections, everyone knows that. But the World Series? Pardon my saying, but you were a nickel and dime operator next to the swells that were in on that fix."

Cudahy shook his head as he poured a shot of whiskey for a patron. "Yer like everyone else, Teddy, in the dark. Maybe it's better you stay that way." Cudahy seemed to be staring right through him.

"No, tell me, man! I want to know. How'd you get in on the caper?"

Cudahy lowered his voice a few octaves. "Do you recall the main guy behind it all, the one who supplied the dough?"

"The big gambler from New York, the Jew, Rothstein. Arnold Rothstein."

"Right. Well, he backed the deal, but the fix wasn't his idea. It was my boss's idea."

"Yer boss."

"Right. Around 1917 I started workin' for a guy name of Sport Sullivan. Ever meet him?"

"Heard of him."

"Biggest bookie in the Hub. A real dandy, and Teddy boy, he could charm the money belt off Shylock, by Jesus. In some ways he was a lot like yerself."

"I take that as a compliment."

"Sure an' that's how I intended it. Well now, Sullivan had his finger in a lot of pies. If there was any action to be had on any sporting event in the Northeast, he was in on it."

"But the World Series is a national thing —"

Cudahy held up his hand. "And aren't you the doubting one? Just listen. Sullivan and I were out for a drink one evening near Fenway Park towards the end of the '19 season. By this time, I was his right hand man. I was especially valuable at, ah, reminding those who were a bit tardy on their payments, ya might say." His lip curled into a chilling wolf's grin.

"I take your drift," said Teddy.

"So like I said, we're at this saloon near Fenway one night and the Chisox are in town for a series with our boys. It's around mid-September. Chicago's well on the way to clinching the American League pennant. A few of 'em come into the bar and they're a little loud; they let everyone know who they are. Typical jockstrappers.

"Well, their table is right near us, and we can hear a few of 'em bitching about the owner, Comiskey. Said he hadn't made good on bonuses he owed 'em and that he's a miserable skinflint in general. Then one of 'em, turns out it was Chick Gandil the first baseman, says he wouldn't mind throwin' off a couple games to stick it up the old man's ass— that is, if he were paid for it. A couple others agreed.

"That's where Sport stepped in. 'Seized the moment,' as he would say. He sends over a bottle of Jamesons, then goes over himself to meet the boys. They were impressed at his credentials, but a little embarrassed we'd heard 'em talkin'. Except Gandil and Swede Risberg, the shortstop. Mother of God, those two didn't give a tin shit about anything.

"Sullivan tells 'em supposing he could get the dough together, what would it take for each man, and how many men would be needed to throw the Series? When he finds out he realizes that to pay 'em off he needed much more cash than he had available. That's when he went to Rothstein in New York. They had a conference and Sport, he told Rothstein that the Series was in the bag if Rothstein would put up the money to pay off the Sox. They wanted ten grand each to fix the games. Rothstein said no dice, that if people found out he was involved they'd know the fix was in and the odds would drop. Sullivan agreed and suggested to let him act as the go-between. That way nobody'd suspect.

Before the Series, remember, the Sox were heavy favorites.

"Well, at first Rothstein turned him down flat. But then he must've realized the possibilities because he changed his mind. He gave Sport $80,000 to distribute to the ballplayers. I was with him when the dough showed up. Let me tell you, boyo, I turned white when the money hit the table. I'd never seen so much loot, not anywhere, not never. So Sport, he takes out thirty G's and tells me to go back up to Boston and put it down on the Reds. See, he was usin' Rothstein's money to place bets for himself! Pretty sharp.

"So, like I said, he hands me the dough, and —"

"And you disappeared."

"Well, not exactly. I put some of it down. I was supposed to place two separate bets for twenty and ten, but after the first one I asked meself, will I ever see this kind of dough again? Not bloody likely, I figured. So I took off. I laid low, got meself a phony passport and shipped out. Didn't tell nobody I was goin', not even you. But believe me, it's better you didn't know."

"And Sullivan?"

"Oh, he made out okay, and Rothstein, and everybody else but the ballplayers, as you well know. See, I wasn't the only one. Everyone in on the deal started tryin' to screw the others. That's how the story broke; somebody who got cut out squealed to the Feds. The ballplayers, bunch of dumbasses, took the fall. Shit, most of 'em never even got paid off. 'Scuse me." Brendan worked his way quickly down the bar, drawing fresh pints and mopping the hardwood. In a few seconds he was back to continue his tale. "So now yer askin' yerself, if he made off with ten thousand smackers, where is it? Jesus and why is he workin' in this godforsaken hole in the wall. Am I right?"

"Well, yeah."

"I lost it, or at least most of it, on the way back over here. It gets boring on a boat ride, boyo. There was a large poker game. It went on fer days. The guys asked me to play, maybe because I was shooting off me mouth so much and acting swellheaded. So I sat in. What the hell, it was found money, and besides, I was just goin' to use a portion of it for wagering. When the smoke cleared, I stepped off the ship with a little over a grand. That was eight years ago, and the grand is long gone. So here I am, runnin' the family saloon, eking out a living. I'll tell ya, Teddy, money can make a man do crazy things. Insane things. But I'm not so sure I wouldn't do it the same way again, if the situation presented itself. Truth is, despite all that happened I want to go back to the States again. But I'd have to go back a wealthy man, if only to straighten out me debts. I've just got to find a way to get me hands on some jack. Jesus and don't you wanna go back someday, Ted?"

"You've got no idea."

"Well then, our course is clear. Do ya believe in fate, Teddy boy? Because the guy I threw out of here as you were comin' in was my sole employee. You need work and a place to stay, I suppose?"

"For certain."

"Fine, then. You can tend bar for me, help me clean up and whatnot, and you can have the room in the back. There's a cot and a sink with running water, not much else, but what the hell? Beats sleepin' in Phoenix Park. What do you say? I'm sure the wife won't mind."

"You're *married?*" asked Teddy incredulously.

"Sure and why not? Good lookin' guy like me with this beautiful establishment here? What woman wouldn't kill fer this?"

The two men laughed raucously.

"Well now, do we have a deal? You want to work with me?" Brendan stuck out his hand.

Teddy grabbed it the way one might clutch a life preserver. "It's a deal, pally."

"Good!" Brendan again dropped his voice low and leaned across the bar so they were almost nose-to-nose. "Listen, Ted. This pub, this business, it's all just temporary. I figure it'll take one big opportunity for me to make the kind of money I need. I've got a few ideas, irons in the fire that I can't divulge at the moment. But I'll want a partner, someone I can count on. A guy with brass balls like me who'll go to the limit to hit the jackpot. You're the guy, Ted. I can use your gift of gab and your talent to think quick in a tight spot. Stick with me and we'll make our fortune and return to the States, an' we'll live high on the hog like we always dreamed of, an' stuff everybody else. What do you say?"

"I'd look the right idiot to turn you down. I'm for anything you want to do."

"Who's the *culchie*, luv?"

Teddy turned at the sound of the feminine voice behind him. He quickly removed his cap when he laid eyes upon the most beautiful woman he'd ever seen. She was raven haired with green eyes that were a shade from being too far apart, and pouting lips that mesmerized him. Despite her common clothes, she appeared to be slim and firm and her breasts strained against the simple cotton shirt she wore. Teddy had never been struck speechless before a woman—until now.

"'E's no *culchie*, dearie. This is me old mate Ted Clancy, just back from the States. Mr. Clancy, meet me better half, Maureen."

Teddy took her hand and shook it delicately, the way he'd learned to do it in the States. "A pleasure, ma'am," he said, flashing his winning smile.

"And isn't he the proper gentleman? What gives here, Brendan, this isn't like your usual crew."

"Teddy's special," he said.

"Is he, now? And what brings you to our humble place of work, Mr. Clancy?" she inquired, clearly teasing him.

Teddy recovered enough to answer, "A job, Mrs. Cudahy. It seems that your husband is looking for a new barkeep and —"

"And where's Duggan?"

"Threw him out on 'is ear," said Cudahy. "Caught him with his fingers in the till, I did."

"I see." She chewed on her lower lip and eyed Teddy curiously. His heart pounded.

"You've got to excuse Maureen, she's a pain in the arse to all me friends," apologized Brendan.

"Who are mostly good for nothings, a bunch of hoodlums they are." She fixed her luminous eyes on Teddy. "I suppose he'll be takin' the spare room?"

"If you don't mind, girl dear."

"Whatever." She dismissed Clancy with a wave of her hand. "Well, I'm off to the green grocers. Be back soon. You'd best show our Mr. Clancy around and give him the ins and outs of the place. Ta-ta." And she was off. The row of barflies turned in unison to watch her go

"Quite a woman," said Teddy finally.

"A wild one, boyo. I guess you could say we're a match. She don't back down from nothin' or nobody."

"She's quite beautiful."

"And isn't that the fact, which is another reason I want you working for me. She don't come in here much, stays upstairs mostly, but I'll feel better knowing someone I can trust is keepin' an eye on her."

Jesus and why didn't they send the devil? thought Teddy.

Chapter Eight

Dublin

The days passed and Teddy fell comfortably into "the bar life" as he called it. Brendan would come downstairs shortly after sunup and wake him. Together they would air out the pub and sweep up any leftover sand used to cover any gastro-mishaps of the previous night's hard-drinking customers, as well as cigarette butts. Once that was done, they had the rest of the morning to themselves. This was usually spent roaming the streets of Dublin, dropping in on Cudahy's "connections"—predominantly bookmakers, small-time hoods and the like. Teddy was gradually introduced to the seamier side of Dublin. And he came to realize that although Brendan was a small-timer in every sense of the word, he was well thought of because of his experience in the States.

The two of them would walk for miles, proposing schemes and shooting them down almost as quickly. Then, it was back to the pub for the midday opening. Brendan came and went, "running errands" as he put it, but Teddy spent pretty much the whole day and night there, swapping stories, sweet talking drunken patrons out of fights, and drawing pint after pint after pint. The only breaks in his day were when Maureen brought down his lunch and supper. He came to look forward to these brief encounters, though she did little more than set his plate down on the bar and move along. When she did move, however, the clientele, which included some of the toughest rivermen in Dublin, cut her a wide berth. Brendan Cudahy was a feared man. Despite this fact, more than once Ted caught himself thinking about her at night. Since no women frequented the pub, Teddy found his social life, which had

46

blossomed in Boston, as fruitless as when he was imprisoned on his brother's farm.

One morning's wanderings proved to be quite interesting, for it revealed much to Teddy about his companion. They were bouncing along, discussing the possibilities of fixing the Irish Derby, when they suddenly found themselves at the gates of Prospect Cemetery. "Come with me," grunted Cudahy.

They followed a meandering path to the top of a rocky hill. The sun was peeking through the clouds and the setting, all things considered, was quite lovely to Teddy. Brendan abruptly stopped for a nondescript gray tombstone. It read:

Sean Cudahy

1856-1916

A True Irish Hero

"Me father," muttered Brendan. "He died in the Easter Rising. Well, after it."

"He was in the Citizen Army?"

"Aye, one of the leaders." He turned his head and spat. "What a travesty that was. Oh, they started with high hopes and ideals, they did. Aimed to create a new Republic. So my da and the other leaders, Connelly and Clark and Pearse—they organized close to 2000 men who believed like they did that Home Rule was a sellout to the Brits. They figured they had to do something dramatic, so the people would flock to their side in a fit of patriotism. But they underestimated the general public"—he spat again—"because they got hung out to dry."

"How so?"

"Well, like I said, they planned the rising for Easter. And it caught everyone by surprise. They took over the General Post Office and a few other key buildings around town and proclaimed an Irish Republic. And that's about as good as it got, boyo, because the Brits brought in heavy reinforcements and bombarded the shit out of 'em. Nobody came to help them out. In fact, the good Dubliners was cheerin' the British reinforcements."

"But why?"

"Well, maybe because so many Irish were off fighting in the English army in Europe at the time, I don't know. So the Citizen Army got embarrassed, and big chunks of the city got blown apart.

"Afterwards they arrested the ringleaders. They took me father off to Kilmainham Prison, gave him a bogus trial, and shot 'im, just like that. And the sad part is, it was all fer nothin'. A few years later, we went through a civil war because we still couldn't agree on the Brits. More shooting. More bombing. And what for?" His eyes glistened.

"You were in the States when he died."

"Yeah. Missed the whole bloody Rising. Me mother took over the pub, but it ran her into the ground. I got back just in time to see her die. I poured the last of Sport Sullivan's money into her damned hospital bills.

"That's why Ireland ain't nothin' to me. People talk about me father now like he was some kind of martyr. What a load of bollocks. They're all just feelin' the guilt fer not helping 'im. Every time some drunk raises a pint in the bar and says, 'May you die in Ireland,' I feel like puking. I say, get me out of this place. I want to go back to America in the worst way. And by God, nobody's gonna stop me."

He calmed himself and turned to face Teddy. "I've got an idea. Been workin' on it a long time. A way we can make more than enough to go back and live comfortable. Something that'll shake these so-called nationalists right down to their shoes, too."

"What is it? A bank job?"

"Better. A kidnapping."

Teddy felt his skin tingle. This was way out of his league, but he was nevertheless intrigued. "Who?" he whispered.

"Not a who. A *what*. We're gonna kidnap something that's so valuable to this country—especially now—that these people can hardly put a price on it."

"And what's that?"

Cudahy's eyes narrowed and his lip curled into a sneer. "The Book of Kells," he said.

"Go on, ya big—"

Brendan pulled him close by the lapels of his jacket and hissed, "Don't ever doubt my resolve, Teddy. I mean what I say. Yer with me, ain't you?" His tone was menacing.

"Of-of course, pally. But...the Book of Kells? How do we get at it?

Isn't it kept at Trinity College under lock and key?"

Cudahy relaxed his grip, even brushed off Teddy's jacket a bit. "Indeed it is. Which is why tomorrow, I want you to wander over to the library, where they keep the book. Get the lay of the land. Let me know about security and the like. I've got some work to attend to on my end."

"All right."

"And not a word of this to anyone, Ted. Not even Maureen."

"Come on, now," said Clancy, chuckling nervously. "We're pals, ain't we? Why in the name of Jesus would I talk?"

"Of course ya won't, Teddy boy. Because ya understand, I'd have to kill ya if you did," he replied, then turned on his heel and the left Teddy alone among the tombstones.

*   *   *   *

Teddy went through the rest of the day in a fog. The magnitude of what Brendan was proposing overwhelmed him. Sure, he wanted to hit the big time, but stealing the Book of Kells was almost unfathomable. "Like a Yank pinching the bloody Constitution," he muttered as he sopped some stout from the bar. Of course, he couldn't tell Cudahy that. Not after he'd seen just how emotionally unbalanced the man was.

The next morning found him at the gates of Trinity College, some three blocks from the pub. A tour group of American students from Columbia University had come to see the book and he blended nicely with them. Though in his early thirties, Teddy had the kind of boyish face that would be forever young. The collegians were shown around the cobblestoned campus and its hallowed halls of learning until they came at last to the long hall of the library, where the main attraction was on display in its gleaming glass case. Teddy eased into position near the front of the group as the tour guide—a small, wiry man with waxy skin and bony hands—went into the familiar drone of one who had recited this address many times:

"Here, ladies and gentlemen, we have the ancient Book of Kells. It dates back to the time when barbarians were attacking the British Isles and brought their brand of paganism with them. Some Irish monks decided that to stem the tide of heathenism they would sail for England and bear into that distressful country the light of Christian learning.

"London at this time was a haunted Roman ruin on a hill, with the brambles over London Wall and the campfires of the East Angles shining in the marsh beyond the city, which they were afraid to enter; Paris was a desolation, and the sun was setting over Rome. But Armagh, the religious capital of Ireland, was the center of European culture. During the three darkest centuries of English history, Ireland was saving Greek and Latin culture for Europe. It was from Ireland, by way of Iona and Lindisfarne, that sandy little island off the Northumberland coast, that Christianity came to the north of England.

"At the beginning of this time an unknown Irish monk was writing the Gospels in an abbey at Kells in Meath, founded by St. Columba. He was one of the world's greatest artists. In the Italy of the Renaissance, he might have been another Michelangelo. He enriched his book with a thousand fantasies and a thousand beauties of intricate design. He poured into this book all the power of his imagination. Men looking at it today wonder not only at the fertility of his brain but also at the keenness of his eyes. How is it possible that a man, unless he employed a type of magnifying glass unknown in his day, could pen such microscopic designs, so perfect that sections of them no larger than a postage stamp when photographed and enlarged show no flaw in the intricate interlocking of lines and spirals?" He paused for effect before his entranced audience.

"This great relic of Irish art was placed in a costly gold shrine. Later in history, a thief stole it from the sacristy of the Abbey of Kells. It was found two months later in the earth. The thief had taken it for the golden shrine and so the book, carelessly flung away, was miraculously recovered, and remains the most perfect expression of Christian art that has survived from the Golden Age of Ireland.

"It is in the Book of Kells that Ireland's remote past lives gloriously in subtle line and perfect color. When a man turns the pages of this great book he turns back the centuries to a world of Irish saints, of Irish poems, of Irish legends, of Irish ships sailing over the sea, taking the light of the Christian Church into the dark places of the world. Are there any questions?"

"How much is it worth?" asked a balding man with horn-rimmed glasses.

"Good question. I will have to answer that by saying that its financial value has never been established. Thousands? Millions? Who knows? The value of this artifact transcends monetary standards. It is, in a word, priceless."

Teddy shivered.

"There must be some insurance premium on it," remarked a bookish woman.

"Sorry, ma'am, you are quite wrong. It is not insured. The college authorities feel, and no doubt wisely, that money could not produce another such book, so that the best insurance is to spend a fraction of the premium that would be necessary on extra fire hoses and watchmen."

"You mean it stays here all the time?" queried a lanky boy with a bad case of acne.

"No, young man. It is removed from this airtight, moisture proof case here every evening and locked in a safe. We're not daft, you know."

There was a chuckle amongst the students.

Teddy peeked over his shoulder at the guards who stood at the doorways at each end of the hallway. Both appeared unarmed. *It'll have to be in broad daylight—pure madness—or we'll be forced to blow the safe it's in at night,* he reasoned. Then it hit him. *I sound the right gangster now, don't I?* Neither plan appealed to him.

Before leaving, he stared intently at the book. It was open, revealing an oversized page of beautiful calligraphy and artistic craftsmanship. Its leaves appeared to be some kind of vellum, and the volume appeared to be quite heavy. He became so engrossed that he didn't realize the group was moving away until they were nearly at the door. At a hurried pace he caught up with them, remained in their midst until they exited the hall, and then disappeared into the streets of Dublin.

Chapter Nine

Boston

Bob Quinn wasn't surprised when he found young Martin the next morning, sitting on a suitcase in front of the Red Sox office entrance. He took the boy upstairs and sat him down. "I've spoken with Mike Connick down in Wilkes-Barre, and they're expecting you. As it turns out, he's in need of another arm. Here's your train ticket."

Martin eagerly accepted the cardboard transfer.

"Now there's just a matter of your contract."

"Contract? What contract?"

Quinn frowned. Boy, was this kid green! "Son, we have to pay you a salary, don't we? I mean, how are you going to secure lodging in Wilkes-Barre? How do you intend to eat?"

"Hadn't thought of that," muttered Clancy.

"Well, so that we can protect you as our property, we are prepared to give you the sum of $200 per month for each month of the season. If I could afford to pay more I would, but we've been having financial difficulties lately." He looked up embarrassedly to find the Irishman beaming.

"Two hundred dollars, sir! That'll be *grand!* Where do I sign?"

Quinn slid a standard minor league contract across the desk to the boy, who scratched out his signature with Quinn's fountain pen. He didn't bother to read it.

"Then it's official," said the relieved owner, standing. "You are now a member of the Boston Red Sox organization, and we're happy to have you. But you've no time to waste if you want to be considered for a roster spot with the big club this season. You have to get to the station and catch your train to Philadelphia, and then on to Wilkes-Barre. You do know where the train station is?"

Clancy shook his head.

Quinn sighed. "I was afraid of that. All right, Mr. Clancy, follow me." And off they went.

* * * *

Although Wilkes-Barre, Pennsylvania wasn't the major city Boston was, it was no slouch, either. Founded in 1769 by John Wilkes and Isaac Barre, two British members of Parliament who supported colonial America, it was formally incorporated in 1806, and grew rapidly after the discovery of nearby coal reserves and the subsequent arrival of hundreds of thousands of immigrants. By 1927, the population was roughly 85,000, many of the newcomers toiling in the anthracite coalmines and Vulcan Iron Works, a major manufacturer of railway locomotives that had begun production in 1849. However, other major companies established bases there as well, including Woolworth's, Bell Telephone, and Planters Peanuts, which had been founded in 1906 by Italian immigrants.

In terms of sports, the Wilkes-Barre Barons were the only professional team for miles, and had an unofficial affiliation with the Red Sox. However, there had been a notable baseball occurrence in Wilkes-Barre in 1926 when none other than Babe Ruth, playing in an exhibition game in Artillery Park, had supposedly blasted a home run that measured off at 650 feet.

Thus, the city where Martin would begin to ply his trade was a hard-working, no-nonsense, blue-collar town of opportunity perfectly suited to the aspirations of the young Irish ballplayer.

* * * *

The train pulled into Wilkes-Barre early that same evening. Martin stepped onto the platform and looked around. There was nobody in sight, save for one man who dozed on a bench, hat over his eyes. Martin walked over and gently nudged him. "Pardon me," he said tentatively, "can you tell me where I might find the Wilkes-Barre baseball club?"

The sleeping man abruptly awoke, blinking his eyes. He was

ruggedly handsome, if somewhat disheveled, and Martin could see they were about the same age. "You Clancy?"

"And there you have the advantage of me," he replied. "Yes, I'm Clancy."

"Bobby Cremins." The young man popped up and extended his hand. Cremins was raw boned but not quite filled out. His close-cropped blonde hair and twinkling blue eyes gave him a youthful look that Martin suspected would stay with him forever. And his posture—chest thrust out, shoulders thrown back—projected a cockiness that reflected a tremendous inner confidence. "They sent me here to meet you, seein's how I'm a rookie on the team. The guys call me Lefty but Bob'll do, too. You'll like the club. Swell bunch of guys. Say, are you a southpaw?"

"Sorry, I don't follow."

"A left-hander. Are you a lefty like me?"

"No, I bat and throw right-handed."

"Swell!" They marched off towards town. "You need a place to stay, Marty?"

The Irishman was taken back at the American's familiarity. No one had ever called him Marty before. "Uh, yes," he answered.

"Well, you can bunk in with me if you want. We'll split the rent. My bed's big enough for two. What are they paying you?"

"Two hundred dollars," he said proudly.

Cremins stopped in his tracks. "That's all? Cripes, that Quinn is cheap. I'm getting three-fifty!"

Suddenly, Martin's salary didn't seem so princely.

The two ballplayers walked through the gathering dusk. "Wilkes-Barre is very different from Boston," said Cremins. "Nowhere near as modernized. Just a big steel mill town. All day long, there's this hazy, sooty cloud overhead from the factory smokestacks. And lots of tough customers. The mill workers don't particularly care for the ballplayers, and vice versa. Gotta watch yourself." They skirted puddles in the unevenly unpaved street. "I got my tryout with the Red Sox late last season. I'm from Pelham, New York. Ever hear of it?"

"No."

"I pitched for my high school team. Did real good. Then I was pitching semipro in the area and I got introduced to Joe McGinnity.

Heard of him?"

"Yes, I've read about him. 'Iron Joe,' right?"

"You got it. Well, he taught me a new pitch, kind of a 'drop'. That put me over the hump. So anyway, the Sox liked me and invited me to training camp in Bradenton. That's in Florida, ya know. I did all right. They sent me out to this place to start the season but I'm going up to the big club this year, I'll guarantee you. Well, here we are. My palace!"

They ascended the stairs over the grocery store where Cremins had his room. A jumble of thoughts flashed through Martin's head. This Cremins talked faster than anyone he'd ever met! And he certainly wasn't lacking in confidence. They entered a small but surprisingly neat room. Martin's spirits lifted at the sight of their bathroom. *Anyplace with indoor plumbing can't be that bad* he thought.

"We played Scranton today," said Cremins. "Lost 5-4. But the season's just starting. I'm pitching tomorrow. You can have the dresser over there. Cripes, I'm hungry. Want to grab some dinner?"

Martin was famished. "Sure," he said.

The two ballplayers visited a local hash house where the bill came to $1.50, including two pie a la modes for dessert. Cremins could see that the kid from Ireland needed lots of help. He didn't know what a hotdog was, or how to leave a tip. Cripes, it was a wonder he knew how to use a knife and fork!

After dinner, they stepped outside. Wilkes-Barre was eerily quiet. Cremins snapped his fingers. "Hey, I got an idea. Since this is your first night here, let's celebrate. How about a picture show?"

Martin was excited. He'd heard about the moving pictures but had never seen one. "That'd be grand, Lefty," he said, "but I've no money left."

"You can pay me back when you get your check. C'mon, it's on me! There's a Chaplin film over at the Majestic. If we hurry, we can catch it."

As they settled into their seats with a bag of popcorn—which Martin loved—a feeling of excitement came over the young foreigner. Thank the Lord that he'd found Lefty Cremins. He was about to express these feelings to his companion when the lights went down. There were scattered "Sssh's" in the audience. Then the piano player began his overture and a funny little man with a cane and mustache appeared on the screen. Martin sat, transfixed, for the entire film. He wished it could go on forever. In fact, the entire day had been wonderful. He'd signed a professional baseball contract, had a ride on a train, made a friend, found a swell place to live, eaten a delicious steak, watched his first moving picture—and tomorrow he would get to play baseball! The only reason he got any sleep at all that night was his sheer exhaustion.

* * * *

The next morning Lefty and Martin ate a hearty breakfast at the same hash house and then moved off to the ballpark. Wilkes-Barre Memorial Park sure wasn't Fenway. In fact, it was falling apart. But Clancy didn't care. Cremins, a thoroughly outgoing sort, brought Martin around and introduced him to the other players as they straggled in. Some didn't look too good. When Martin asked Lefty about it, he got this advice: "Listen, Marty. This team's like most other minor league clubs. Half the guys are on the way up, trying to make the Bigs. The other half, on the way down. Maybe they were in the Bigs at one time but they're not good enough anymore. So, they're hanging on. Some for another shot. Some just for a paycheck. We got a few drinkers on this club. Spend all night in a saloon or pool hall, piss away all their money. Not me. I don't drink. Don't smoke. If you listen to me you'll stay away from that crowd." Indeed, some of the veterans, especially the pitchers, were pronouncedly cool to the newcomer. He was an interloper, a threat. Cremins continued his lecture: "The other group you gotta avoid is the card players. They get a hold of green rooks like yourself and steal 'em blind. Our money comes too dear to throw it away. Steer clear of 'em."

Martin again thanked his lucky stars for his new friend Lefty.

The new recruit was issued a high-collared uniform that was too big and had a few holes, but at least the spikes fit this time. He was surprised at how threadbare his uniform was compared to the one he'd tried on in Boston. In fact, the entire clubhouse, if one wanted to call it that, couldn't hold a candle to Fenway. It was damp, the roof leaked, and his 'locker' was an open stall with a chipped wooden stool in front. A couple of nails were hammered into the inside of the stall for him to hang his clothes.

His introduction to manager Connick was curt. "All I can tell you, son, is keep your nose clean, be on time, and stay on my good side. Have Cremins here show you our signals. Our pitchers go out early on game and practice days to work on their pickoff moves and bunting. And you'll take your turn pitching batting practice. So don't ever be late. When Lefty's not pitching, sit next to him on the bench. He's got half a brain, so keep asking questions. That's how you learn."

Martin nodded. The man's personality was chillingly like his own father's. "When will I get a chance to pitch, sir?" he asked innocently.

"When will you get a chance to pitch?" The manager was incredulous. "When I'm damned good and ready to put you in, that's when! And cut out that 'sir' shit. It's 'Skipper' from now on or I'll fine you. Got me?"

"Yes, Skipper!"

"All right, then. Lefty, are you ready to hurl today?"

"You know I am, Skip!" sang out Cremins.

"Well then, get your butt outside and get loose!"

The two youngsters fairly ran out of the room, Cremins chuckling under his breath. When they reached the dugout, Martin grabbed him. "Lefty," he said, "I've got to ask you a question."

"Shoot."

"What are signals, pickoffs and bunts?"

Cremins laughed aloud. "You really don't know?"

Martin shook his head in embarrassment.

"Marty, stay *real* close to me," he said.

That fine spring afternoon Martin Clancy witnessed his first baseball game, and it was a beauty. Lefty was cocky and in control on the mound. Martin noticed how the catcher mixed up fastballs and curves, setting up the hitters. He watched Lefty glance over his shoulder to keep baserunners close to the bags. He listened intently to the southpaw while their team was batting. Besides pitching well, Lefty seemed to be a pretty fair hitter also, twice batting safely in four chances. The game ended, 4-1 in favor of Wilkes-Barre. Cremins went the distance and was congratulated by all as he left the field. The crowd, which numbered about 200, was generous in its applause also. As the two pulled off their flannels afterward, the dour clubhouse man, who had the odd name of

57

Smiley, collected their garments, which were heavy and stank with sweat. These would be hung out to dry overnight. Washings took place every week or so.

"Got any questions?" asked Cremins, pulling off his spikes.

"Just one. Remember in the fourth inning, when you allowed those two baserunners?"

"Yep, what of it?"

"Well, the other team was really yellin' at you, calling you horrible things, like 'mick' for instance."

"Yeah, so?"

"Am I to take it that this conduct is within the rules?"

Cremins was taken back. "Of course it is, Marty! It's all a part of the game. Hey, we gave it right back to them. And it'll get worse. Wait'll you hear the kind of things they yell at us when we're on the road. That includes the fans, y'know. And sometimes they throw things, too."

"Such as what?"

"Vegetables, bottles, whatever they feel like. But it's all a part of the trade. Hell, 'mick' is the mildest of things you'll get called. But the key is, Marty, to keep your own crowd on your side. If they applaud you, tip your cap. Always make it look like you're trying, even if you're bushed. And if they do get on your back, never, *never* let them know it bothers you. If you show your feelings, then you're sunk."

*   *   *   *

Two weeks came and went. Martin took batting practice with the team and threw some also. He worked on fundamentals with Lefty. Then game time would roll around and he would assume his customary seat on the bench. As he watched the Wilkes-Barre Barons in action, he began to realize that in the minor leagues individual performance was put above winning. As long as the team played .500 ball, Connick seemed to tolerate it, but Martin found it hard to accept.

The first road trip, as all that would follow it, was arduous. The team bus, which was driven by Connick, left Wilkes-Barre at dawn and arrived in Elmira, New York many hours later. The players barely had time to dress and warm up, and it was time to play. Afterwards they piled into the bus, stopped for a greasy box dinner of hamburgers and fried potatoes, and arrived at the fleabag hotel they would be staying at for the next couple of days as night fell. It was totally without the glamour Martin had anticipated as he read about the exploits of his heroes back in Ireland. In fact, he was getting damned frustrated about not pitching. When was the Skipper going to give him a chance?

The next day Lefty and Martin arrived early from their walk to the visitors' clubhouse. "Well, looka-here," said Cremins, reaching into Martin's stall. He plucked a new baseball from Martin's empty spiked shoe. "Connick's calling card. You're starting today, my friend."

A flock of butterflies took wing in the right-hander's stomach, but Martin quickly brought himself under control. His plan was to make believe that he was throwing to Uncle Ted on the farm. He would pay no mind to the batter or the crowd. After a brief conference with his catcher and a few words of encouragement from Cremins, he was raring to go. He threw strongly in pregame warm-ups, and the catcher, a grizzled veteran named Walenski, remarked to Connick that the kid had good command of his pitches. He'd have to prove it now under fire.

Martin Clancy took the mound against Elmira with grim determination. He smoked his eight warm-up pitches. The umpire brushed off home plate, assumed his position behind the catcher, pointed to Martin and yelled, "Play ball!"

Walenski put down a single digit for the fastball, pounded his mitt, and set himself. Martin double-pumped, rocked and kicked...and heaved the ball over the backstop. Spectators scattered. The Elmira bench fell over themselves in laughter as the batter, catcher, and umpire followed the flight of the ball into the stands.

"He's just nervous," said Cremins aloud.

Martin grimaced as the catcher tossed him a new ball. The batter stepped in again, gingerly. He was scared to death. Walenski put down another number one. This time Martin's offering split the plate.

"Stee-rike!" bellowed the ump.

Walenski nodded, smiled, and snapped the throw back to his pitcher. Clancy was on his way. He was to throw only eleven more pitches that inning, most of them for strikes. The third batter posed the biggest threat, tapping weakly to the mound. Martin easily scooped up the ball, took his crow step, and threw him out. The dugout was all smiles as he pounded down the steps. "Good job, Marty!" said Lefty. "That's the way to mow 'em down! Now we have to get you some runs."

But the runs didn't come easily for Wilkes-Barre this day. A single in the first inning was wiped out by a double play. Clancy bounded back onto the field after only a few minutes' rest. And so it went. Both pitchers hung goose eggs on the ramshackle scoreboard for the first four innings. Neither team could get any kind of rally going. Even Martin's clean single in his first at-bat in a ballgame was wasted, as his teammates then made outs.

Martin faced his biggest challenge in the sixth. With nobody out, their leftfielder hit a slow chopper wide of first base. Timoney, Wilkes-Barre's first sacker, ranged to his right to backhand the ball. However, Martin was so engrossed in the action that he failed to cover first base, forgetting his responsibility on this fundamental play. Temporarily flustered, he subsequently gave up a ripping double down the right field line. Once again, he was hurt by a mental lapse. As the right fielder dug the ball out of the corner, Clancy should have been sprinting to back up third base. But he stood rooted to the mound as men scurried in all directions around him. The right fielder's throw short-hopped the third baseman and ricocheted over his shoulder into the Elmira dugout. The base runner was awarded home plate and Martin was behind, 1-0.

It was at this time that manager Connick made his first trip to the mound. He looked past the boy, appearing to be searching the horizon for ships. "Are you tired, kid?" he asked.

"No, Skipper! I feel just fine. I would very much like to continue."

Walenski joined the conference, his catcher's mask tilted back on his head. "He's still humming 'em," he volunteered, and spat a glob of tobacco juice.

"All right then. But if you start getting shelled I'm yanking you."

Martin blew away the next three batters on ten pitches and sailed through the last three innings without any difficulty. But the opposing hurler, a crafty old-timer, allowed no runs at all. And so, in his first baseball game, Martin found himself on the short end, despite tossing a three-hit gem. He was understandably glum afterward, but remembered to tip his cap to the sparse crowd, who respectfully applauded. He was further buoyed when both Connick and Lefty congratulated him for his fine effort.

That night in Elmira, while most of their teammates were out drinking, the two pitchers took in a film and afterwards discussed Martin's mistakes over chocolate sundaes. Cremins said, "Old Connick was really impressed with you today, Marty. I wouldn't be surprised if he's talking to Quinn right now about the two of us."

"Do ya think so, Lefty?"

"Sure. Marty, don't you realize that Boston's a pathetic club? Look here." He pulled a piece of newspaper from his wallet and unfolded it. "I cut this out of the *Sporting News* the other day at the barber's. The Red Sox are picked as a 50-1 shot to win the pennant. They're in the cellar already!" He leaned forward and whispered conspiratorially, "They can't help but bring us up eventually. We've just gotta keep doing good. Forget about the goof-offs on this team. You and me are going places!" He popped a maraschino cherry in his mouth and grinned.

Chapter Ten

Dublin

"No Wild West show for us, boyo," said Cudahy as the two men placed chairs upside down on tables. "We can't be sure the guards ain't packin' pistols, and what's more, we'd bring the whole stinking police force down on our heads. We've got to go another route."

"Blow open the safe?"

"Nah. There's another way. One I'd hoped to avoid. We've gotta bring in a third man. A good cracksman, to get us inside that safe. An' I know just the man; he lives in the North, just outside Belfast. We've never worked together but we have mutual acquaintances. Question is, whether he'd do it, and what we'd have to pay." He moved to the bar and poured them another shot of whiskey. They drank them down. "Tomorrow, I'll head up there to meet with 'im. You take over while I'm gone. Christ, you practically run the place anyway."

"Are you going to tell Maureen where you're goin'?"

"Nah, I'll make something up. She knows better than to ask questions. I'll be back in a couple days. Keep yer eye on her."

"Surely."

"Right. Okay then, I'll be off early t'morrah." He poured them another shot and they downed them. "To success," he said.

"Success," Teddy repeated.

The next day was business as usual. Teddy awoke, aired out the pub and toured. He avoided Trinity College because he did not want his face to become familiar to the staff. Instead, he crossed and re-crossed the bridges that spanned the Liffey, stopped for a cup of tea, and pondered

62

his future. He began to think about Martin, how he was faring in America, and how disappointed the boy would be if he learned his uncle was in cahoots with a man who'd been involved in the Black Sox scandal. He pictured himself in the grandstand at Fenway, surrounded by friends, a beautiful woman at his side, pointing to the pitcher's mound and proclaiming grandly, "That's me nephew Martin. Taught him all he knows!" He decided to contact Monsignor Garvey to find out about how Martin was doing. After asking directions, he found his way to the closest Western Union office and sent a wire to Garvey:

DEAR MONSIGNOR—HOPE THIS MESSAGE FINDS YOU WELL—PLEASE SEND INFORMATION AS TO MARTIN'S PROGRESS—HOPE TO SEE YOU SOON—TED.

He left the pub's address with the clerk and headed back across the Liffey. Then, the day continued as all days. The regulars came and went, the crowd swelling at closing time of the factories and again after dinner. It was payday and business was brisk.

Maureen seemed in a peevish mood. She'd been nicer to him lately, even calling him Teddy a few times, but today she was clearly perturbed, no doubt due to Brendan's sudden departure. He wondered how in the world they ever got together. But then again, despite his romantic adventures in America, there was still so much about women he did not understand.

That night he closed up by himself. Afterwards he sat at the bar, pulled out a bottle of Bushmills and a glass and poured himself a stiff one. Teddy was not much of a drinker, but he did enjoy a taste or two now and then. Cudahy, on the other hand, often went past his limit, especially when drinking with his pals. He could be a mean drunk, too.

Clancy was turning towards the back to retire for the evening when there came a tapping at the pub's front door. "We're closed, mate," he called out.

Another tap-tap-tap.

"Christ," he muttered, and strode to the entrance. He unlocked the door and was surprised to find Mrs. Brendan Cudahy, framed by the streetlamp light.

63

"I must talk to you," she said curtly.

Teddy was off balance. "Yes, all right, sure," he managed as she blew by him and toward the single light, which burned in his quarters. His quarters!

When they reached the room, she whirled on him, her eyes blazing. "All right now, where is he, Ted?" she asked matter-of-factly.

"Why, I've no idea—"

"You're lying. I know you two are up to something out of the ordinary. And he's tryin' to keep me in the dark, but I'm too sharp for that. Now, I'm staying right here until you tell me." She removed her cape and stood there, arms folded across her chest, feet spread in a combative stance. The swell of her breasts as she breathed drove him mad.

"Now Maureen, Brendan would be upset with me if I were to betray his trust—"

"Trust!" she wailed. "Trust? What does he know about trust? He doesn't trust *anybody*. Not you, not me."

"That's not true, Maureen."

"Bloody hell it isn't. Hasn't he told you to keep me under surveillance?"

"No, I—"

"Then why do you watch me so closely?" Her voice softened. "Is there something that catches yer fancy, perhaps?"

"Of course not! I mean—"

"You're saying I'm not attractive, then?" She arched an eyebrow.

"You are very pretty," he answered. *Hail Mary, full of grace, here am I, a sinner,* he thought.

She began to unbutton her high-collared shirt. Slowly. Her eyes never left his. "I know you've been watching me, Ted Clancy. I can feel yer eyes burning into me when I walk past. I don't mind." Her blouse hit the floor. Teddy couldn't take his eyes off her lace corset, which barely held her inside. She stepped out of her shoes and started on the buttons of her woolen skirt.

"Brendan's a terrible man. He treats me very poorly. Do you think it's easy for me, living in this place, existing amongst the vile men he calls friends, acting like some kind of indentured servant? I'm merely a possession to him. A shiny bauble he can show off to his pals." There was a rustle of fabric as her skirt slid to the floor. She moved toward him.

In a full panic, Teddy spluttered, "Pardon me for asking, 'cause it's none of me business, but why in the world did you ever marry him?"

"A good question and I'll answer it. Because I was a young girl who wanted to get away from her father and Brendan was the bold, strong son of an Irish hero who had ambitions for grand things. And of course, I believed him. In a word, I was stupid. Didn't know what I wanted. But I know now."

Teddy Clancy, famed ladies man of Boston, was quite excited to feel his knees nearly buckling as she took a pin from her hair and shook it out. It flowed well past her shoulders and shone in the light of the naked bulb.

She stood before him and her eyes reached into his, pools of hypnotic green that beckoned to his wildest desires. "Am I beautiful?" she asked huskily.

"Yes."

She brushed his lips with hers once, twice, and they locked into an embrace. Her darting tongue teased him and made him want much more. Teddy, who had never been one to exhibit great amounts of willpower, was quickly overcome. "Turn out the light, lover," she purred, "if you're up for a real woman."

Teddy had made love to many ladies in his role of self-styled Boston Casanova, but his encounter with Maureen went beyond the depth and scope of his experience. She was an unquenchable hellion who pushed him to his limits of ability and stamina. They writhed in the dance of love, her occasional cries punctuating the stillness of the night.

Some hours later, as they lay sweat-soaked in the small, cramped room, she traced circles upon his chest and nuzzled his ear. "Lover," she said soothingly, "you don't have to tell me what yer up to, not right now. But promise me that when the hour is close you'll let me know."

In the afterglow of their passion, Teddy would've promised her the world. "Sure an' I will," he whispered.

"Good," she answered. "And we'll both keep quiet about all this, won't we? We wouldn't ever want that nasty Brendan to find out. No tellin' what a barbarian like him might do." She said no more. There was no reason to. She took his hand and kissed his fingers. "Now, love me again," she said.

Chapter Eleven

Wilkes-Barre

The chilly, sometimes downright freezing days of April gave way to the milder climes of summer as the Wilkes-Barre ballclub plodded through their schedule, winning one here, losing one there, never rising above their comfort zone of mediocrity. With every passing day Martin learned a little more, whether it be an obscure base running rule, the strategy behind a pitchout, or something as interesting as American slang. He did his best to try to speak in the popular vernacular, while toning down his Irish brogue as much as was humanly possible. He discovered that he liked jazz music, hot dogs and movies of all types. He disliked chewing tobacco, asparagus, and the embarrassingly forward young ladies who harassed the ballplayers. For the most part, he and Lefty remained somewhat removed from their teammates, which he sometimes regretted, although God knows some of them were going to kill themselves carousing. One thing was understood, however: Clancy and Cremins would give a one hundred percent effort every time out. And in so doing, they earned the respect of even the crustiest, most jaded veterans.

By the end of July, both pitchers were sporting fine records. Lefty had amassed an impressive 12-3 slate, and Martin had a respectable 6-4 mark. He had lost his first three outings, due mostly to mental errors, but had gone on a 6-1 tear afterwards in which his earned run average was under two. The Irishman was more the power pitcher of the two, averaging one strikeout per inning. Lefty, on the other hand, gave up some runs here and there, but seldom when they counted. He put the ball in play and let his fielders take over.

A strong bond was formed between the two young hurlers. They spent entire days together and never seemed to tire of one another's company. Lefty, a natural leader, was delighted to have a young novice such as Martin to introduce to the many facets of baseball and American life. And Martin, for the first time in his life, had a friend his own age whom he could talk to and dream with. And while it's true that baseball players are somewhat akin to battlefield soldiers in that they shy away from deep attachments that can suddenly be terminated by trades or career-ending injuries, Lefty and Marty seemed to thrive on shared experiences and interdependence. Their inseparability and likeness in stature and ancestry led them to be known in the clubhouse as the "Tipperary Twins."

But Lefty was chafing more and more as the days drifted by. He constantly complained to Martin that the Sox were hopelessly mired in last place and that neither one of them could do any worse than the pitchers with the parent club. "Cripes, what're they waiting for?" he would lament.

"Don't worry, Lefty, our chance is coming," Martin would counter soothingly.

"So's Christmas."

Martin hated times like these, because Lefty would get himself so worked up that he'd threaten to quit. "I can just pack up and leave anytime I want," he'd say. "I'm good with a pencil and paper, you know. I can get a job as an artist with the newspaper or a magazine. I don't need this aggravation."

Clancy knew his friend was right, for Lefty was always whipping off quick sketches and caricatures of teammates that were both hilarious and accurate. The thought of Cremins leaving scared Martin to death. But sudden goodbyes have and always will be a part of baseball, and a familiar scene played itself out on a stifling August morning in 1927.

Martin was dead to the world, face down on his pillow, his sheet pulled over him more from habit than from necessity. Even though it was 92° and there was no air-conditioning, he could not get the memory of those cold, damp Irish nights out of his bones. He was dreaming of his father rousing him to milk Amy when he realized that it was not Mike Clancy but Cremins who was shaking him.

"Marty, Marty wake up! Cripes, how can you sleep in this heat?"

"The Irishman turned over and yawned. "Jaysus, Lefty," he grumbled, "it can't yet be seven o'clock. What're ya waking me for?"

"I've been called up."

Martin's eyes snapped open and he sat bolt upright. "Yer having me on, Cremins," he said warily.

"Honest to God," he answered. "I just got the message from Connick. Quinn wired him last night, and he sent the message over with Smiley. I've gotta pack and catch a train to Boston. I'm going to the big leagues!"

"Just like that?"

"Yeah, just like that. I don't even have time to say goodbye to the guys. I'll stop by in the clubhouse and pick up my glove and bats, and off I go."

"I'll come with you." Martin quickly dressed as Lefty stuffed clothes in his suitcase. He kept glancing over at the American, wishing he would straighten up, slap his knee and crack, "Had you going, huh?" But this was no joke. And it was all happening so fast.

They went downstairs and out into the humid sunlight. It was going to be another scorcher. By the time they reached the ballfield, Lefty's jacket was soaked. He packed his equipment in a duffel bag. No words were said. In fact, neither man talked until they had reached the railroad office. "One way to Philadelphia," said Lefty. He pocketed his ticket and turned to Martin. "I'll transfer at Philly and go to Boston from there. The Sox are just beginning a homestand."

"Yes. A homestand," repeated Martin, as if in a trance.

Cremins looked to the heavens. "Cripes, Marty, don't make me feel bad about getting my break. You look like a lost puppy! Jeez, you'll do all right. You've saved up your money so the rent's not a problem. Remember, don't let the landlord charge you over fifty cents a day. And you know where to eat and have your clothes cleaned."

"I'll be fine, Lefty. It's just that—"

"I know, I know. We're a pair. An odd pair, but we go together. Listen, you'll do fine. Just keep winning. Before you know it, you'll be up with me on the big club. I'll put in a word for you with Carrigan, you know that."

"I know."
"And whatever you do, stay away from the goof-offs!"
"I will."
Cremins looked at his watch. "Listen, it's half past eight. You gotta grab some breakfast and get to the ballpark. Our game with Harrisburg is at two. So get going, or Connick will have your head."

An uncomfortable silence passed between them. In the distance, maybe five miles off, could be heard the sound of a locomotive, drawing inexorably nearer. "You'd better go," Cremins repeated. The two shook hands. Then Martin turned on his heel and walked back to town, his footsteps echoing through the empty streets.

*　*　*　*

The next day, Martin trudged along, hands thrust deeply into trouser pockets, through the streets of Wilkes-Barre. Today's game, the second of the homestand, wouldn't begin for hours, and he was trying to come to grips with being alone. Lefty's departure yesterday had really hit him this morning, when he'd awakened to an empty room. He so missed their friendly banter as they took turns shaving before the bathroom mirror—though his baby face hardly warranted it—and the discussion of what adventures the day would bring. He'd even gone without breakfast, stopping only for a cup of coffee, which he was beginning to prefer over tea, at the corner place where they usually took their meals.

"Where's your buddy, hon?" the heavyset counter waitress had queried as he settled onto a stool.

"Gone," was all he could muster. He'd finished quickly to escape the prying eyes of the usual morning patrons.

The current heat wave was still in effect, the humidity so thick he could touch it. And yet, he kept walking, past factories and cheap hotels, grocery stores and warehouses. A cloud of industrial smoke hung above him like a canopy, filtering the sun. If Martin Clancy had ever been more miserable, he couldn't remember when.

Then, as he turned a corner a sound came to him, strains of violin music so plaintive it sounded like someone crying. He stopped momentarily to concentrate on the melody. Though he couldn't identify its name or composer, he realized that it perfectly captured his melancholy. He decided to track the music to its source. Halfway down the street he found it: a small eatery with the sign *Garofalo Ristorante*. The entrance was open, and the sweetly sad arrangement wafted into the street from its dark interior. Judging the time to be roughly 11:00 AM, some two hours before he was due at the ballpark, he boldly decided to venture inside and solve the mystery, and maybe see if they could make him a sandwich.

It was immediately cooler once he crossed the threshold, and as his eyes adjusted, he could make out eight small, circular tables with a few chairs apiece, a simple bar, and a doorway leading to the kitchen. Colorful paintings of rustic European scenes dotted the plastered walls, and each table featured a red and white checkered tablecloth with candleholders fashioned from empty wine bottles. Overall, it was a cozy place, a place where—

"May I help you?"

Martin, startled, took a step back and a girl emerged from the shadows, violin in hand. She was much smaller than he was, barely over five feet, but not frail. Her dark brown hair was pulled back on the sides and fell in long tresses down her back. And though she was simply dressed in a high-collared blouse and long skirt, he could tell that a full figure lay beneath. "I—er—sorry, ma'am, you must be closed. I'll be leav—"

"If we are closed, then why did you walk in?" she asked, playfully arching an eyebrow.

"Well, ah, I heard the music," he managed, motioning to her instrument. "You play wonderfully."

Despite the gloom, he could see the blush in her cheeks. "Thank you," she said. "I'm happy you could enjoy it."

"Have you been playing long?" he asked.

"Since I can remember. It is my greatest happiness in life."

What an odd thing to say he thought. "My name is Martin, Martin Clancy. I'm with the Wilkes-Barre club."

"Club? What club?" she asked, clearly confused.

"Oh, sorry," he smiled. "The local baseball club. The Barons. We're professional," he proudly added.

"I see. Well, Mr. Clancy, I am Lucia Garofalo, and this is my

71

family's restaurant. We feel it is the finest in all of Wilkes-Barre, but you'll have to judge for yourself. You...did come here to eat, yes?" Her eyes, a dark brown, were both friendly and appraising.

"Yes, of course," he said.

"Well, unfortunately, we are closed until five o'clock."

"Oh, well, I see," he stammered, feeling the right fool.

"But that does not mean I could not make a sandwich for you." She gestured to a nearby table with delicate, tapered fingers. "You would like to sit?"

"Yes, please." He pulled out the chair and eased into it. *Why am I sweating worse in here* he wondered, *and what on earth should I order?*

As if reading his mind—and panic—she offered, "I am sure that in the kitchen we have some salami and provolone cheese. Would that be sufficient?"

At this point, he would have agreed to sawdust on toast. "That would be lovely, miss."

She lay her violin and bow on the bar and drifted toward the kitchen, stopping short of the door to look back over her shoulder. "You will not run away while I am gone?" she teased, again arching an eyebrow.

"Wouldn't think of it."

"All right, then."

Martin exhaled deeply as the door snicked shut behind her. She was, indeed, lovely, if a bit mysterious, though she seemed to be his age. But what on earth was salami?

He didn't have to wait long to find out. The girl returned, with what seemed like the longest loaf of bread he'd ever seen, stuffed with a dark red meat and fragrant cheese. A glass of earthy red wine the likes of which he'd never tasted accompanied this. The girl began polishing the bar, casting an occasional glance back at him as he devoured the meal. He was torn between a ravenous hunger and a desire to spend as much time as he could watching her. Even while cleaning the bar top her movements were fluid and graceful.

"I think you like salami," she said finally, clearing the table.

"It's grand," he said with a smile, comfortable for the first time. "How much do I owe you?"

She chewed her lip thoughtfully. "Seventy-five cents should cover it, but there is no charge."

"No charge?"

"Not if you promise to try our restaurant for dinner sometime soon."

"I'll be back for dinner tonight, after the game!" he blurted like a schoolboy.

"Well, if you like. But please don't feel obligated. Complimenting my music was enough to earn you a free lunch. But, only once. Next time, you pay."

"Yes, ma'am."

"Miss Garofalo is sufficient."

"Miss Garofalo," he repeated, careful to pronounce the flowery name correctly. He rose, awkwardly, and backed out of the entrance, nearly falling over a chair and a nearby table. The last thing he saw as he reentered the blinding sunlight was the inscrutable smile of the olive-skinned beauty. He walked to the ballpark with a spring in his step, wondering what delicacies awaited him upon his inevitable return.

Chapter Twelve

Dublin

Teddy reached out for Maureen. He cupped a soft, white breast and she moaned passionately, her fingers tightening in the curls at the back of his head. Suddenly she gripped his shoulders. Hard. What strength this woman had!

"Teddy! Wake up, boyo!"

Clancy's eyes bolted open and focused on the florid face of Brendan Cudahy, who was shaking him. "What? But—" he spluttered.

"Relax, man, it's me. I'm back. You were havin' yerself a wicked dream, you were. Thrashing around like a stuck pig! You all right?"

Teddy shook the cobwebs and looked around the room. "What time is it?" he asked groggily.

"Well past midnight. I just got back to town, but I had to speak to you, I'm so excited."

Clancy sat up and yawned. "What is it then?" he asked, stretching his bones, which were still sore from his workout with Maureen.

"I met with our man yesterday in a ruined church in South Belfast. 'E seems to want to avoid crowds. An odd duck, our cracksman. Anyway, I told him what we were aiming to do and he thought I was daft, of course. But you could tell he was interested. I mean, who would ever figure a caper this big?

"We agreed that he'd come down and examine the safe where the book is kept. He'll have to steal into the college, which he said is no problem, and determine the nature of the beast he'll be dealin' with. Once he figures that out, he'll give us a price."

"Sure and how do we pay it?"

Brendan flashed his broken smile. "I tol' ya to let me handle that part of the deal."

"When's he coming down to case the safe?"

"Monday next. Let's see, that would be five days from now."

Teddy thought hard. "Now where do I fit in?"

"You, my good friend, are going for a job interview tomorrow. The Sexton of St. Michan's Church is retiring, and William Stafford, the vicar, is looking for a replacement. That would be *you*."

Teddy was incredulous. "Me, a *churchman*?" he cried.

"Simmer down, simmer down, boyo," Brendan whispered, the smell of whiskey heavy on his breath. "The problem with you is, you don't think I've any dense matter up here," he said, pointing to his forehead. "I've been planning this for a long time, I tell ya. The thing is, we're gonna need a place to hide the Book of Kells while we make our ransom demands. St. Michan's is the perfect place."

"And why is that?"

Cudahy chuckled. "Oh, you'll find out. Just be there at nine t'morrah morning. Stafford knows yer comin'. I've told him all about me favorite cousin, Connor."

"Connor?"

"Connor O'Shea, you are. From Ballyshannon. Can you remember that?"

"Sure."

"That's all I told him about you, except of course you'd be perfect for the position. You can fill in the rest as it comes up. You're good at that."

"But hold on a minute. I've gone past that church. Isn't it Anglican?"

"That it is, boyo."

"But we're Catholics, aren't we?"

"Right again."

"So how did you get mixed up with the Anglicans?"

"It's like this. After the Rising, and the execution, the pastor of our church apparently turned his back on me mother. Spoke ill of her husband—said he'd been guilty of stirring up the masses and promoting violence or some such nonsense. Well, that did it for her. Meanwhile, a friend of hers put her on to the Vicar Stafford, who offered some solace in her time of need. It was like heresy to some people, y'know, turnin' her back on her religion, but she didn't care. My ma was a tough old bird." He sighed. "Actually, the Vicar's not a bad sort—for an Anglican. What the hell, put a collar on 'em and they're all the same."

Teddy frowned. This was all going so fast. His mind wandered to his brother Mike, fast asleep in his bed after an honest day's work. For a fleeting moment, he envied him.

"Something wrong, pally?" Cudahy's voice snapped him back to reality. "You don't look too hot."

"Been workin' hard, I guess," said Teddy.

"Aye. I just looked in on Maureen, and she said you've been hard at it since I left."

Teddy swallowed as he searched Cudahy's eyes for suspicion. He found none. "Lots of customers. Payday, you know."

"I take your drift. Well, t'morrah you get yourself over to St. Michan's and meet the good Vicar. It'll do you good to get out of this dump for a spell. G'night."

As Cudahy closed the door behind him and locked up, Teddy staggered to the bar, pulled out the Bushmills and poured himself a stiff one, the bottle clicking against the rim of the glass. He downed three successive shots before the shaking stopped.

Teddy Clancy, adulterer... gangster... church sexton? *Mother of God!*

Chapter Thirteen

Wilkes-Barre

Garofalo Ristorante took on a completely different air at night. Sounds of laughter beckoned to Martin from within, and the cooling of the day kept his dress shirt from wilting. As he poked his head through the door, he was struck by the warmth generated by the wine bottle candles that threw shadows upon the paintings and the flowers stenciled along the tops of the walls.

The girl stood, notepad in hand, chuckling as she took the order of an older couple at one of the far tables. She looked his way, nodded slightly, and seemed to smile. Was she actually happy he'd returned? She gestured toward an empty table near the bar and he seated himself, straightening the tablecloth. After what seemed like hours, she finally made her way over to him. "Ah, the return of Mr...." She looked to the ceiling playfully, as if struggling to remember.

"Clancy."

"Yes, of course, Mr. Clancy the *professional* baseball player."

Now it was Martin's turn to blush.

"Would you like to see a menu, Mr. Clancy?" she asked.

"Indeed, yes."

"Then I regret to inform you that we do not have one. However, I can tell you the dinner list for tonight. We are serving spaghetti with oil and garlic, rigatoni with meat sauce, *chicken cacciatore*, and *beef bracciole* over *risotto*. What would you like?"

The Irishman, completely panicked, stared at her. "Er, I don't know what any of that is," he mumbled.

"The *chicken cacciatore* is a specialty of the house," came a low, rumbling voice from behind the girl, causing the color to drain from her face. Easing her aside, a man stepped forward, his eyes serious as death. He was of average height and barrel chested, with a fringe of grayish hair above his ears and dark eyebrows. Though attired in a white shirt and black trousers, he also wore an apron tied around his waist and his sleeves were rolled up, revealing muscular arms and scarred hands that had seen much work. "I welcome you to my restaurant. I am Giuseppe Garofalo," he said with a stiff bow. "I see you have already met my daughter, who likes to play games." He glanced sideways at her, and the girl seemed to shrink before his eyes. "You are needed in the kitchen, Lucia," he snapped, dismissing her; then he continued, "This is your first time here?"

"For dinner, yes," Martin managed, receiving a suspicious look in response.

"You are from town?"

"Actually, no, sir. I play for the Wilkes-Barre professional baseball club."

"Oh, I see. A ballplayer." He made it sound vaguely insulting. "Well, I have been here since 1920, when my late wife and I opened the business. Before then I worked in the Planters Peanuts factory in town. You have heard of them?"

"Sorry, I haven't."

Garofalo raised a bushy eyebrow. "You are not from the area, then?"

"No sir, not hardly," Martin replied, wary of this line of questioning.

"I see. Well, as I was saying, my Francesca died two years ago. Lucia, my daughter whom you have met, runs the business with me."

"It's a grand place," offered Martin.

"We are proud of it. I built it from nothing." He seemed to puff out his chest as he said it.

"I am looking forward to your chicken, then."

Finally, Garofalo came close to smiling. "Lucia will bring it." He made his way back to the kitchen, pausing at each table to check on his patrons, many of whom seemed to be regulars.

Martin exhaled. This man was downright frightening, especially when compared to his daughter. But then, she seemed fearful of him as well. He munched on a piece of delicious crusty bread and awaited the return of the girl. Finally, she emerged from the steamy kitchen, holding aloft a plate of chicken in gravy, swerving gracefully between the tables until she set it before him. The fragrant brown sauce set his mouth to watering, but when he looked up to express his satisfaction, he could see she was clearly distressed. He knew immediately that some kind of reprimand had been issued in the kitchen, rendering her expressive face impassive and cold.

"Would you like some wine with your meal, sir?" she said tonelessly.

"Yes, that would be wonderful." She retreated to the bar and poured Chianti from an earthenware jug into a wine glass. He thought he saw some moisture in her eyes, but couldn't be sure it wasn't the candlelight playing upon her face. Or maybe it had been the heat in the kitchen. Only by convincing himself of this could he fully enjoy the meal before him.

By the time she cleared away his plates and brought his coffee, the restaurant had pretty much cleared out. Martin, in the depths of loneliness, desperately wanted to speak to her, but it was clear such fraternization had been prohibited. As he paid his bill, he could see past her into the kitchen entrance, where the door seemed to be left ever so slightly ajar. "Did you enjoy your meal, sir?" she inquired stonily.

"A fine meal, miss." The blood was pounding in his ears, but Martin fought through it and whispered, "May I see you sometime?"

She paused and swallowed. "I work here every night, six days a week," she replied evenly. "Thank you for your patronage." She turned on her heel and retreated to the kitchen. Martin pushed in his chair and left, the chicken sitting in his stomach like a bag of baseballs.

*   *   *   *

The next day began a long homestand, commencing with a series with the Delaware Valley ballclub. Martin made sure to pass by *Garofalo Ristorante* on his way to the ballpark. As was the case the previous day, Lucia Garofalo's sorrowful sonata drifted to the street where he paused at length but dared not enter. The last thing he wanted, either for himself of the girl, was to face the menacing visage of Giuseppe Garofalo. With a pang of regret, he continued on to the ballpark.

79

The games came and went, tedious affairs that featured uneven, sometimes listless play on the part of his teammates. Of course, whenever Martin was called upon, either as a starter or relief pitcher, he became totally focused and gave his all. Each day introduced another nuance of the game, and he concentrated intently from his seat on the bench, shying away from the practical jokes and aimless banter of the ballplayers, most of it centered around carousing and women. Always lurking in the back of his mind was the promise of another night where he might interact with the mysteriously enchanting Italian girl.

Martin had never been in love, nor had he shown much interest in the females within his social circle in Cashel. He found them plain and unexciting, with nothing to look forward to but the grueling existence of rural housewifery. But this beautifully exotic girl was somehow *alive*; he detected a fire smoldering within her, and in his flights of naïve fancy saw himself taking her away from this sooty industrial city to a life of luxury as the best girl—or maybe even wife—of a major league ballplayer in a big city. It was America, after all, and anything was possible. Uncle Teddy had told him so.

And so, the young pitcher presented himself, cleaned up and smiling, at the Italian restaurant night after night. When Lucia would see him enter, she would glide to his table, a basket of bread at the ready, and relate the evening's specials. And though the food never failed to be intriguing and expertly prepared, what he savored most of those few stolen exchanges with the girl, which despite her efforts to disguise it, were pleasant for her as well.

On the third night, he asked again to see her. Unfortunately, within seconds the omnipresent Giuseppe began making his rounds. Martin was sure he was done for, but she whispered, "Kirby Park, tomorrow morning at ten o'clock. I can't stay long."

"That'd be grand," he found himself replying to her back as she moved away from his table to avoid the approaching proprietor.

"You come here every night," said Garofalo, his swarthy face a mixture of distrust and curiosity. "You like my food that much?"

"Oh, yes, it's wonderful, sir," he replied politely. "Best I've ever had."

"*Graci*," said the owner. "The selection is simple but fresh. My

80

daughter visits the market each morning for the ingredients. Someday this will all be hers." He gave a nod and moved on, leaving Martin to wonder if there was a message for him in there somewhere. As he left the restaurant, he caught her eye one last time and offered a furtive wave, and was elated to see it returned.

*   *   *   *

The next morning threatened rain, and Martin hoped it would hold off until he had met with Lucia. He cleaned up and then ate a buttered roll with coffee at the hash house. Then it was off to Kirby Park, the soles of his shoes slapping the pavement. He arrived way too early for his 10 AM appointment, and made himself comfortable on a park bench near a duck pond. The air smelled like rain—something he was well-versed in. His heart thudded as the minutes passed. Finally, he asked a well-dressed, middle-aged man out for a morning stroll what the time was.

"Ten-oh-seven, young man," he replied before clicking shut his silver pocket watch. "You waiting for someone?"

"I was," he answered dejectedly. "Thanks all the same."

The man sauntered off and Martin, defeated, stood and stretched. He guessed the most direct route to the ballpark and he was turning to go when the girl, carrying a cloth grocery bag, entered the park, casting glances left and right as she moved. She was dressed simply, with a peasant blouse and skirt cinched tightly around her trim waist, but he figured she'd look grand in any attire.

"I can't stay long," she warned. "I am supposed to be at the market."

"I understand," he replied, smiling broadly. "Would you like to walk a bit? Here, let me carry that bag for you." He held out his hand and she hesitantly gave it over.

They began an awkward stroll, and more than a minute of agonizing silence had ensued before she broke the ice: "You said that you are with the Wilkes-Barre baseball club?"

"That I am," he replied, trying to mask his excitement over the fact that she'd actually remembered their previous conversation. Then he forgot if he'd formally introduced himself, so he did it again. "Me-my name's Martin Clancy," he said, stopping to shake her hand.

She took it, gently, and fixed him with big brown eyes. "I believe you mentioned that. And I am still Lucia Garofalo. Pleased to make your acquaintance, Mr. Clancy."

"Please, call me Martin," he said.

"As you wish. And you may call me *Signorina* Garofalo."

"Sin-what?" he stuttered.

And then she laughed, a wonderful soft chuckle that calmed him. "I'm only joking," she said. "I take it you're not from around here."

"No ma'am. Actually, I've only been in the States for a short while. I'm from Cashel, in Ireland."

"I see. And you've come all this way to play baseball?"

"It's how I plan to make my career," he answered proudly.

"Ahh," she replied enigmatically.

"I'm actually fairly good at it," he said with a hint of defensiveness, as he could not read her so far.

"I'm sure you are, Martin. I'm told the Wilkes-Barre Barons are a successful team."

"You've never taken in a game, then?"

She shook her head. "I have no time for games. My only recreation, I'm afraid, is the violin."

"You play beautifully."

"Yes, well, you've said that already."

He felt like he was sinking fast. "Your father told me he expects you to take over the restaurant someday."

"Did he? Well, that's the first I've heard of it, but I suppose it makes sense."

"Is it what you want to do?"

"What I want to do?" She chuckled to herself. "No, Martin. What I want to do is become a famous concert violinist and travel the world, playing to great crowds and gaining national acclaim."

"Then we have something in common."

"Which is?"

"To dream of playing before great crowds and gaining national acclaim, like you said."

"Martin," she said gently, "I'm afraid for me it's nothing but a fantasy. Perhaps it is more realistic for you."

"I hope so. The Red Sox—they're in Boston, you know—they signed me to a contract, so I'm more or less their property. I'm hoping that if I do well down here, they will notice and call me up to the big club. It's the hope of all the players down here, I guess."

"So that's the way it works. I often wondered. Other ballplayers have come into the restaurant over the years. It's hard to keep track. The faces change every spring. They come and go." She shrugged.

"Does your father not approve of you speaking to ballplayers?" he asked uncertainly.

"My father does not approve of me speaking to *anyone* without his permission," she replied. "Since my mother's untimely death he has taken it upon himself to shield me from the world." There was a trace of bitterness in her voice. "His plans for me, made without my consent, do not include the company of transient ballplayers."

Martin swallowed hard. "My father also had my life planned out for me," he said resignedly. "That's why I left, Lucia. I couldn't bear the thought of plowing fields for the rest of my life." They walked a few more steps and he said, "If you could, would you just pack up and go?"

"As you did?" she replied, the words stinging him. "No, I could not do that. It would kill my father." She pulled a small, brass plated pocket watch from her skirt. "Pardon me, but I must go," she said.

"Could I walk you back?" he offered.

"No," she said, reaching for her bag, which he regretfully handed back. "That would not be prudent. If we are seen in town there could be trouble."

"Seen by your father?"

"Or his friends. Word travels fast in a small town like Wilkes-Barre."

"Can I still come for dinner tonight, after the game?"

"That's up to you, Martin."

"But would you *want* me to?"

She regarded him with a sweetly sad look. "The special tonight is *zuppa de pesce*," she said.

"What's that?"

"Don't worry," she said with a smile as a stray drop of rain caught her on the forehead, "you'll love it."

Chapter Fourteen

Dublin

Vicar Stafford proved to be a far different personality from Teddy's old buddy, Monsignor Garvey. He was reed thin, with pomaded black hair combed straight back. Hollowed cheeks and a cottage cheese complexion gave him a cadaverous look. However, he did possess a rather dry sense of humor. When Teddy came upon him in the church, he was attending to the task of polishing the oaken pulpit, a white apron tied around his waist and covering his floor-length cassock. They exchanged pleasantries and Stafford discarded his apron before settling into a pew with the prospective sexton. "So you're Connor O'Shea," he began. "Brendan Cudahy recommended you, am I correct?"

"That's right, Vicar. E's me cousin."

"An odd one, our Brendan. A hot-tempered bully at times. Rather well known in these parts, and for all the wrong reasons. But he did love his parents. That's when we became acquainted, at your aunt's funeral."

Clancy stiffened. He didn't know the name of Brendan's mother. "Aye," he managed, "she was a good woman."

"None finer. She came to us after the Easter Rising, and of course, we welcomed her. It's a pity she's no longer around to counsel him. Lord knows he could stand some good advice."

Teddy didn't answer.

"I take it you're Catholic, like Brendan?"

"Yes. Is that a problem, Vicar?"

"Well, it doesn't affect whether you can do this job, I suppose. We serve the same God. You've no qualms about mingling with us humble

Anglicans?" He gave a wry smile.

"None whatsoever."

"Good man yourself. Too much emphasis is put on religious differences anyway, if you want my opinion. It's one of the things that divides us as a people." He sighed and looked around the church's interior. "Right. Well now, as sexton your main task will be to deal with the tourists, show them around the place. Brendan said you'd be perfect in that capacity. Said you really spewed out the Blarney. That's what the tourists expect, you know. And I don't see any harm in accommodating them."

"I agree totally," beamed Teddy.

"Good. Heaven knows the ladies will take to you, but you must also possess a knowledge of the grounds. Let's take a stroll around the church." As they began to walk, Stafford started the narration that Teddy would have to repeat morning and afternoon from now on. "St. Michan is said to have been a Danish bishop who founded the church about the year A.D. 1095, on the site of an ancient oak forest, though some have argued that he was actually an Irish martyr. The church was initially Catholic until the Reformation. The current church dates from 1686, the only parish church on the north side of the Liffey surviving from a Viking foundation. There isn't much to see in the church proper; it's rather plain when compared to some of the more ornate Catholic cathedrals. If you look towards the back, you'll notice a Stool of Repentance, which was used for some kind of public trial and confession. Only one like it in the whole of Ireland. Pretty odd piece. The pulpit I was working on when you came in can be swung round to face any section of the congregation. No one escapes my gaze." He chuckled at his own joke. They came upon a monstrous pipe organ along a side wall, adorned with gilded cherubs. "Handel is said to have practiced his 'Messiah' on this instrument before the first performance in Dublin," said the cleric proudly.

Pretty boring, thought Teddy.

"You're thinking it is rather run of the mill, aren't you," said Stafford, expertly reading Clancy's face.

"Well, to tell the truth, Vicar—"

"My boy, the show is only beginning," smiled the clergyman.

"Come along."

They exited through the churchyard and approached heavy metal lift-up doors at ground level of the outer wall of the building, which rested upon a slanted cut stone sidewall built into the church's foundation. Stafford produced a huge key and snapped open the equally large padlock that secured the portals. He turned to Teddy. "Before we go down, let me tell you why St. Michan's is so well-known. People come here to look at the bodies."

"Bodies of what?"

"Of people, lad. In the vaults beneath the church. They are preserved by some peculiarity of the atmosphere as perfectly as any Egyptian mummy. It is a touch morbid and horrific, but it is unique in Ireland, if not the entire world. Are you still game?"

"Lead on," was Teddy's reply.

Stafford lifted open the doors and they began down a steep flight of stone steps into the darkness of the charnel house. Teddy was surprised to notice that the air was not chilled or clammy as it would be in a typical crypt. In fact, it was quite comfortable and surprisingly fresh. "Best air in Dublin, some say," shot Stafford over his shoulder, again reading Teddy's mind. Once at floor level, Teddy looked around as Stafford adjusted an electric torch. A handful of high vaulted cells led from each side of a central passage running east and west beneath the church. Each was fitted with an iron gate.

"Let's see who's about," said the clergyman, obviously enjoying himself. He swung open a wrought iron cell gate and flashed the torch upon a sight so ghastly that Teddy nearly wet his trousers. Coffins lay stacked one on top of another, almost to the ceiling. It appeared to be the vault of a noble family. Lords and ladies, generals and statesmen lay around them in human strata. The last coffin placed in position rested upon the others like cordwood. The lower coffins were of a shape and color long outdated. Some, which bore coats-of-arms, were covered in red velvet, which had not decayed much or faded in color. Others were bound in black leather, and studded with big brass nails that showed no trace of tarnish.

When Stafford began to speak, Teddy nearly jumped out of his shoes. "If you look closely you'll notice that the weight of the dead pressing on the dead has caused the coffins to collapse into one another, exposing a hand here, and arm there, and so forth. The fascinating and somewhat gruesome feature of all this is that these men and women, some of them dead over five hundred or more years, haven't gone to dust. They're like mummies. Their flesh is the texture of rough leather. Stranger still, their bone joints work. Observe!"

Teddy looked on bug-eyed as Stafford flexed and straightened a protruding leg as if it were his own. He moved along to another chamber where a lone coffin lay open against a wall. The corpse inside rested with one leg crossed over the other. Stafford gazed upon the occupant. "Traditional death posture of a Crusader. Means he'd been to the Holy Land. Shake his hand, lad!" Clancy examined the nails of a man who had been dead for nearly 800 years but could not bring himself to grasp the hand.

The two men ventured from vault to grisly vault. In one, Teddy saw the body of a woman, said to be a nun, whose feet and hands had been amputated. "Tortured," was Stafford's only comment.

And so it went. Who knew how many hundreds of bodies were down there, how many generations of families, stacked upon each other like American pancakes? The only living creatures were spiders who had spun webs of immense size, some reaching from ceiling to floor in certain vaults. "What do they live on?" asked Teddy.

"Themselves, lad. Men who study spiders and the like come here from all over. Cannibalistic insects, or so I'm told. Oh, and another thing. You've heard of the writer Bram Stoker?"

"Of *Dracula* fame?"

"One and the same. It's said that a visit to these vaults gave him inspiration for that macabre tale."

"But how can the people—the bodies down here—stay so, so human?" Teddy wondered aloud.

"Well, the generally accepted theory that explains their remarkable state of preservation is the air in the vaults is chemically impregnated by the remains of the oak forest which stood here in ancient times. That and the fact they are made of limestone. So long as the vaults are kept totally dry, decay ceases. Should only a little moisture enter, the results would be disastrous. All the bodies would crumble into fine dust. Then what would we have to show our tourist friends?" He smiled his undertaker's grin. "Let's join the living and have a cup of tea, what say?"

"Best offer I've had yet," said Teddy thankfully. They climbed into the chilly air. Even the rain that was falling could not dampen his joy of being out of that grim place.

In the rectory, they arranged for a modest stipend for Teddy, who preferred to keep his quarters at the pub. He would begin tomorrow in his job as cryptic tour guide. "There's no fee, of course, for a look downstairs," said Stafford with a sly grin, "but feel free to tell our guests that a donation to St. Michan's would be greatly appreciated."

"Or we won't let 'em out?" joked Teddy.

"Hmm, a novel idea," mused Stafford.

Teddy accepted the padlock key and happily started home. When he entered the pub, Cudahy burst into laughter. "And so how was it?" he guffawed.

"Pour me a Guinness first," mumbled Teddy.

"My pleasure, reverend," cracked Brendan, and he drew a pint. His voice dropped a few octaves. "So do ya see why St. Michan's is the perfect place?"

"Sure and I do," said Teddy. "Slip the Book into a coffin and it would stay there a good long time without rotting."

"Exactly. I told you, boyo, I've got it all figured out. I didn't let on about the nature of the job as I didn't want you reactin' negatively to the thought of workin' in the crypt. But what the hell, it won't be fer long. An' whenever yer surroundings get depressing, just imagine yerself sailing along in Boston Harbor with a pretty *colleen* on your arm. Someday, boyo, we'll both look back on this and have us a good horse laugh, we will."

Chapter Fifteen

Wilkes-Barre

By the time he had seated himself at his now-usual table some eight hours after the interlude in Kirby Park, Martin was determined to ask the elder Garofalo permission to spend time with his daughter. This bold idea had turned over and over in his mind as he whiled away the afternoon on the bench, waiting for the driving summer rainstorm to subside, though it never did. The teams would simply play a doubleheader the next day.

As always, Lucia greeted him with the breadbasket and a reserved smile. He'd decided not to inform her of his intentions for that evening, and even ordered a glass of Chianti, which he hoped would fortify him for his undertaking. The seafood-laden spaghetti—a heaping portion that he had to fight to get down because of his jangling nerves—was somewhere near his breastbone when Giuseppe Garofalo found his way to the table. "Welcome again," he said politely. "I hope the meal was to your liking."

"Oh, indeed," he replied, his foot involuntarily tapping beneath the table. "Ah, sir, if I might have a minute of your time?" He motioned to the empty chair across the table.

The proprietor sat and looked him square in the eye. "Is there a problem?" he asked suspiciously.

"Oh, no, sir," said Clancy, summoning every bit of Irish charm he could muster, "it's that, I was wondering if, you see, your daughter—"

"No."

"Sir?"

Paul Ferrante

Garofalo's icy stare never changed. "Please do not be offended, son," he said evenly, "but my Lucia does not associate with ballplayers. You may exchange pleasantries if you continue to patronize my restaurant, which is your choice, but it stops there. *Capice?*"

Martin didn't know what the last word meant, but he'd gotten the drift. He nodded dumbly as Garofalo motioned to his daughter, who had witnessed the exchange from afar. "Lucia, an *espresso*, with *anisette* on the side, for this nice young man." He shot Martin one last look before adding, "on the house."

With tears in her eyes, she brought his coffee, the delicate *espresso* cup chittering on its saucer. "Oh, Martin," she whispered.

"Tomorrow at ten in the park?" he whispered back.

She shut her eyes and shook her head.

"Please, Lucia?"

"I'll try."

*　*　*　*

This time Martin was seriously upset. What right had this man to demean a profession he knew nothing about? The man's protectiveness of his daughter was understandable, but wasn't this supposed to be the land of opportunity and equality? Again he arrived early, pulling himself together on the same bench as the previous day, practicing the bold speech he would deliver to the beautiful girl. He realized that perhaps he wasn't being totally rational, but then again, he'd never felt this way about a girl. When she entered the park, groceries in hand, he muttered, "Okay, laddie, here we go," and rose to meet her.

"Let's just sit today," she said, forcing a smile.

"Your eyes are red," he observed. "Have you been crying, Lucia?"

"Yes," she said softly.

"Why?"

"I saw the pain and the embarrassment on your face last night," she said. "I could have told you that it was of no use."

"It's not fair to you," he said, his fists clenching. "You should be allowed to make your own decisions."

"And is it this way in Cashel, Ireland, I suppose?" she asked.

"We are not in Ireland!" he hissed, trying to control himself. "This is

90

America! I thought things would be different here."

She closed her eyes for a moment, her extraordinarily long lashes fluttering. When she opened them again, they were wet. "There is much you have to learn here, Martin," she began. "While it's true this is a place of great opportunity, many people who come here bring the old ways with them. In my culture, the parents, especially the father, have much to say about who may or may not court his daughter. It's not that you're a bad person—far from it. Even an idiot can see the decency in you, Martin Clancy. But there are two things not in your favor. First, you are Irish—or rather, you are not Italian. If my father does not actually pick the boy I shall marry, he will at least limit my suitors to those of my nationality. And second—and I'm sorry if this offends you—my father cannot take seriously one who plays games as a living, especially if the boy in question wants to become serious with his daughter.

"I think you will discover that the life of a ballplayer—even one who is paid well—will be filled with uncertainty. You are moving here, there, and everywhere, making it hard to put down roots. Your teammates will be with you one day, gone the next. And, I suspect that despite the comradeship, and the adulation you seek, there will be times of loneliness as well. Lucia Garofalo, the humble restaurant owner, would not be able to fill your needs."

Martin, trying desperately not to sound irrational, blurted, "Come with me to Boston. We could make it work."

For the first time, then, she touched him, her hand to his cheek. "I don't think you've heard a word I've said," she sighed. "My poor, sweet Martin. Do this for me: go on to Boston, and have a great career. I will look for you in the newspapers, and I will tell people I knew you when you were just an innocent boy, beginning his adventure in America." And then she kissed him lightly on the lips, the first time he'd ever been kissed by anyone but his relatives. "But don't come back to the restaurant—ever," she finished. "It would be too difficult for us both. Goodbye, Martin."

She rose from the bench and walked away He kept hoping she'd look back, but she never did.

* * * *

91

Paul Ferrante

The next day, the last of the homestand, Martin went out of his way to pass the *Garofalo Ristorante* on his walk to the ballpark. From inside he could hear the mournful strains of Lucia Garofalo's violin, and wondered if she would ever play for the man she would someday wed, or if she would ever think back upon the silly Irish boy who wanted to take her away from the life being forced upon her.

But there was one thing of which he had no doubt: never again would someone tell him he wasn't good enough.

Chapter Sixteen

Wilkes-Barre

The bumpy bus ride to Harrisburg had been especially uncomfortable for Martin. By the time they boarded, the conversation had gotten round to Lefty's recent promotion, and whether he was succeeding in Boston. Such information was customarily greeted with a mixture of envy and bitterness. And these bad feelings carried over onto Martin. He felt his teammates stealing sideways looks at him throughout the series as he sat alone. He eventually feigned sleep to escape their stares.

The games were generally tortuous. There was nobody to sit with and tutor him as the contests unfolded. He found himself concentrating on the action so much his head hurt. Thankfully, he fell asleep quickly on the trip back to Wilkes-Barre.

The bus ground to a halt at the ballpark and the team scattered. Martin began the long trek to his rooming house, equipment bag slung over his shoulder. He decided to cheer himself up by going to see a picture, but he was preoccupied during the show. It just wasn't the same without Lefty. He didn't even finish his popcorn.

The next day during batting practice Connick took him aside and slung a meaty arm around his neck. "S'matter kid," he said, "ya look like your dog died."

"Just a bit homesick, Skipper," he replied.

"I understand. You're in a strange country and you miss your folks a little, maybe. And Cremins. Truth be told, I kinda miss him myself. But I'll tell ya, it wouldn't be so bad if you just mix with the fellows a little. They're a fair lot; I've had much worse. Sure, they'll take advantage of a youngster like yourself from time to time, but that's a part of growing up in this game. Hell, these guys gotta play behind you, right?"

"Right."

"So give 'em a chance is all I'm saying."

"Yes, Skipper." Martin appreciated Connick's concern, which went far beyond what he'd come to expect, but he was still wary. Why would Lefty be so adamant about avoiding these guys if they were so grand? He continued to keep to himself for a couple days until he finally broke.

It was a fine Saturday evening. He'd pitched the second game of a doubleheader, shutting out Reading 7-0. He hadn't had his best stuff, but the fellows had performed magnificently behind him, turning three double plays.

Martin dined alone—unless one counts the *Sporting News* as a companion—at a burger joint, and then took a walk through town, giving the Italian restaurant a wide berth. He was passing *Bronko's Billiards Emporium* when a voice cried out from the doorway. He turned and saw the smiling face of his catcher, Stan Walenski. "Well, well! If this don't beat all! It's my battery mate, in the flesh. And after dark, no less."

"'Lo, Stan," said Martin.

The brawny catcher came outside and grabbed his pitcher by the elbow. "Come on in and say hi to the boys, kid. We was just talkin' about what a gem you tossed today." He gave the youngster a theatrical wink.

Martin remembered Connick's advice. "Sure, Stan, I can drop in for a while."

Walenski led the Irishman through the smoky pool hall, populated mostly by mill workers and a few women of dubious appearance. They crossed the billiards room and entered a doorway. On the other side was a small room with bootleg whiskey boxes stacked along one wall, and a circular table around which sat six of his Wilkes-Barre teammates. The place stank of cheap cigars. There were beer bottles and playing cards scattered about the table, and the men were laughing. "Hey, fellows," called Walenski, "see what the cat dragged in!"

A look of shock registered on the seated men, who appeared to be in various stages of drunkenness. "Clancy! It's Clancy, begorrah!" yelled first baseman Brian Timoney in an exaggerated Irish brogue. "Why don' ya sit with us a wee bit, laddie?" The men roared.

"Come on," whispered Walenski, prodding him from behind. "They won't bite ya."

Martin sat down and was handed a schooner of beer. He'd had a taste or two of the stuff back home, mostly on holidays, but was by no means familiar with alcohol, outside of the rich red Chianti sampled at *Garofalo Ristorante*. However, he was too embarrassed to decline this gesture of goodwill.

Walenski stood up and called for order. "Shaddup you guys," he said. "I wanna propose a toast to our winning pitcher in recognition of his fine effort today. To Clancy!"

"To Clancy!" they echoed, and quaffed their brew, slamming their glasses down afterward.

Martin drained his glass. It was more bitter than the sarsaparilla he drank at the ice cream parlor, but it was blessedly cool, and the pool hall was uncomfortably warm. Someone slid another schooner across to him. A discussion started about the day's doubleheader, and he found himself interested in what others had to say about the team and their manager. It seemed that most of the criticism was levied against those not present. He said little, but sipped his beer and listened. They weren't such a bad group, despite what Lefty had said.

"Hey Clancy," said Timoney suddenly. "Stan here says you're probably the strongest player on the team. What do you think?"

"I couldn't say."

"You're too modest, kid," said the catcher loudly. "All that farm work has made an ox out of you. Why, in the ninth inning you were still popping the ball. I had to soak my catchin' hand in ice after the game!"

Martin blushed. "Well, I have done quite a bit of heavy labor in my life," he admitted, beginning to enjoy the warm buzz of the beer.

"Only one way to find out," said Timoney. "Let's let him arm wrestle Bronko!" The others nodded their approval. Martin was pulled to his feet and swept along with his mates to the billiard room where Ladislaus Bronko, the proprietor, tended bar. He was a squat, wide man who appeared to Martin to be chiseled from brick. His eyes were black and far apart and his nose was flat from a lifetime of brawling. He was completely bald. Bronko had a towel draped over his shoulder and wore a dirty T-shirt, which exposed his huge, hairy biceps. A cluster of mill workers sat before him at the bar, slurping their watered-down prohibition beer.

"Hey Bronk," called Walenski, "we got somebody here to challenge you to an arm wrestle."

The group at the bar turned around and faced the ballplayers. "Yeah? Who iss dat?" said Bronko curiously.

"Our star pitcher, Mr. Clancy." They pushed Martin out front.

"This iss some joke, no?" laughed Bronko. "I vill tear hiss arm off. Iss no contest!"

"We got fifty bucks says he can beat you," challenged Walenski. Martin's head snapped around and he looked at his teammates wide-eyed. This was an awful lot of money. He suddenly wished he were somewhere else.

"Fifty dollars! Ho, ho! Iss good! I wrestle him!"

Timoney stepped forward. "And if he wins?"

Bronko frowned and thought hard. "Zen you drink free all night—my best stuff."

"Agreed!"

They sat Martin down at a small table in the middle of the room, removing his jacket and rolling up his right sleeve. "Wait a minute," said Clancy. "That's me pitchin' arm. I won't wrestle with it."

"Are you as strong with your left?" asked Walenski.

"I think so."

"You'd better *hope* so, kid."

Bronko seated himself across the table. When Martin put his left arm up the brute seemed momentarily confused, then shrugged. "Don't matter," he grunted.

The two clasped hands, their elbows on the table. Walenski stood over them, his hands enveloping theirs to keep them upright and steady. "All right," he said, "here's the rules. There's no using your other hand to grip the table. You must stay in your seat. And there's no winner until the back of somebody's hand touches the table. Are you ready?"

"Yes," said Martin.

"Yes," said the Hungarian.

"Then…begin!"

Bronko let go a deep, throaty roar and jerked Martin's arm down to within an inch of the tabletop. Both sides screamed encouragement to their champions, the mill workers pounding on the bar, the ballplayers crying out for Clancy not to surrender. Martin looked into the flat, sinister eyes of the bartender. Bronko's face was contorted in a snarl that chilled him, yet the boy hung on. His many years of working the plow and stacking slabs of peat had prepared him well for this test of brute strength. Beads of sweat formed along Bronko's forehead and trickled down into his eyes, but he refused to blink or wipe them away, intensifying his intimidating glare.

Seconds ticked by.

Then slowly, ever so slowly, Martin began to rally. With each degree of leverage he attained, the wild cheering of his teammates intensified. After nearly five grueling minutes, the wrestlers' hands were vertical again. Bronko was sweating profusely. But Martin was also starting to tire. His impassive face belied the weariness that was creeping into his shoulder and upper arm. What would his teammates say if he lost? How much of the fifty dollars would he have to ante up? The thought of failing in front of them terrified him, and supplied an adrenaline rush such as he had never experienced. He smashed Bronko's fist to the table as the room exploded.

The Wilkes-Barre club pummeled his back and mussed his hair. They bore him aloft and paraded around the room. Bronko, nursing an aching hand, ground his teeth. "A bet's a bet!" cried Walenski triumphantly. "Pay up, Bronk!"

The bartender, smoldering, reached beneath the counter and pulled out four brand-new bottles of Canadian whiskey, clamping them down on the bar with such force that they nearly shattered. The ballplayers grabbed them up and retired merrily to their room in the back.

"Wotta man! I knew he had it in 'im!" yelled Timoney. The others chimed in. Glasses were filled and toasts were drunk.

Clancy, enjoying his fame, drained his glass every time it was filled. He quite liked the warm feeling the liquor induced, but even in his numbed condition, he realized the hour was late, and he had a long walk ahead of him. After many rounds and much procrastination, he decided to go. "Gennalmen," he said, rising, "thanks for a wonnerful evening. I'll be taking my leave of you now." Then he keeled over and hit the floor.

Timoney ran to his side and felt for a pulse.

"Is he dead?" asked Walenski.

The first baseman looked up. "Nah, just passed out." There was nervous laughter among the men.

"Well what're we gonna do with him? Nobody knows where he's living. Where do we take him?"

Timoney grinned madly. "Listen, fellows. I've just gotten a great idea," he said.

*   *   *   *

"Clancy! What in hell are you doing on my goddamn desk!"

The disoriented pitcher, jolted into consciousness, rolled off Connick's chipped office desk and onto the floor, hitting the deck with a thump that was reminiscent of the previous evening. "Ooh, me head," he moaned.

Connick jerked him to his feet by the now-soiled lapels of his jacket. Martin rocked woozily in the manager's grasp, his eyes glassy. "Look at you! You fresh busher, you're a mess! You smell like shit and you puked all over my desk, for Chrissakes! The hell's got into you!"

"G'mornin', Skipper," he mumbled.

"Smiley!" screamed the irate manager. The clubhouse man came running but stopped short when he saw the disaster in the office. "Don't just stand there, you idiot! Get me some black coffee! Quick!" He dragged his young pitcher into the ancient players' bathroom, thrust his head into the sink, and turned the faucet on full blast. The pipes rattled, kicked, and shot forth a jet of freezing water. After a half-minute or so, Connick pulled the boy up to eye level again. Martin, his head a mop of dripping curls, seemed to be coming back to life. "Now," said Connick, "I'll ask you again. What have you been up to?"

"Out with the team...last...night," he managed. "Remember...you said—"

"I know what I said!" raged Connick. "But I didn't want you to get stinking drunk! Look at you. You're a damn disgrace!"

Martin's head was spinning...or was it the room? "I'm sorry, Skipper, please don't shout at me...no more...I just want to sleep...just a bit," he murmured.

Connick sighed. "That's the problem, kid. You *can't* sleep. You've got to catch the first train to Philly. You've been called up."

"Wha—"

"By the Red Sox. They're pulling into Philly this afternoon for a series with the Athletics. You're to meet them there. Today. Congratulations, kid."

Martin was a jumble of emotions. He was happy, embarrassed, frightened and confused.

"I'm gonna send Smiley for your things. Tell him your address and give him your key. Meanwhile, take off all your clothes, they're not worth half a shit. Get a stool, put it under the shower, turn on the water, and sit there until you sober up. You understand?"

"Yes, sir. Could you let me go now, sir? I think I've got to retch again." He staggered off to the bathroom.

Smiley burst into the office with a steaming mug of coffee. "Where's the kid, Skip?" he asked.

Connick pointed to the bathroom. "He's in there. Go get his keys and find out where he's living. Clean out his room." He looked at his filthy desk. "Here we've got this kid who's gotta go up to the big club today, and he's half dead and puking his guts out. What a way to make a living."

Smiley turned to leave but Connick caught him. "Hey," he said, "where ya going with my coffee?"

Chapter Seventeen

Dublin

Fortified by a double shot of Jamesons, Teddy went off to begin his brief career at St. Michan's. He proved to be an instant success, as his talented tongue and charm overcame any morbid fears presented by his workplace. He conducted three tours before and after lunch, spending his break in a nearby park with a sandwich packed by Maureen.

What to do with her? He didn't want to tell her about the plans because he feared Brendan's wrath. Besides, she could only muck up the job. However, he was horrible at keeping secrets, and she would no doubt pump him for information as time went along. And she could be very persuasive. Teddy didn't even want to consider what would happen if Brendan found out about their tryst. He cursed his weakness and wondered what would happen if, indeed, the heist came off as planned.

Supposing they secured the Book, and Teddy hid it in the crypt. What then? How would they ask for their ransom? Through a newspaper, a go-between, or what? And supposing they got their money. Would they be able to slip out of the country? And if so, would Teddy be bound to Brendan and Maureen back in the States? Heaven forbid; a triangle like that could only lead to his doom. He desired Maureen, but self-preservation came first.

He returned home after work, ate dinner, spent some time with the patrons and took a turn behind the bar, then went to bed.

"How was it?" Brendan had asked upon his return.

"Pretty dead today," he'd snapped, and didn't realize he'd made a joke until Cudahy broke up.

"You're a comedian, boyo. Did you sort out a proper place for the Book?"

"That won't be a problem. There's lots of hidey holes."

"Good. Only a few days now till the cracksman comes down to case the safe over at the college."

"If he reports to you that he can do the job, when do we move on it?"

"As soon as possible, aye."

"So, there's a chance we could be doing the job next week or so?"

"Hopefully sooner. S'matter, Teddy, aren't you anxious to get on with it?"

"Y-yes, of course."

"You just be ready when I need you, boyo, and we'll be in Boston come August. Catch some games at Fenway!"

*   *   *   *

The next morning Teddy returned to the church, and the next, and the next, keeping the outward appearance of cheerful goodwill while skidding deeper into depression. He found himself taking a drink at lunchtime to sustain the morning's dose. The liquor didn't affect him outwardly, but it kept him from shaking on the inside. Bad as his current status was, he hoped something would come up that would abort Brendan's audacious plot.

Monday arrived, and Cudahy, in a state of excited anticipation, brought breakfast down to his co-conspirator at the break of dawn. "All right, boyo, tonight our man's comin' in on the eight o'clock train. Me an' him will be taking our stroll over to the college. Then, after he's got the lay of the land we're gonna retire to an out-of-the-way place to discuss things. Can you tend the bar tonight? Maureen will help you out. I've told her not to expect me until morning."

Clancy felt his stomach drop.

"A problem, Teddy?"

"No, none. I'll be here."

"Good man. With any luck, we will hopefully have a plan of attack formulated by tomorrow."

"Listen, Brendan, I can handle the pub meself tonight. It's not

101

necessary—"

Cudahy dismissed Teddy's offer with a casual wave of his hand. "Nah. Let 'er do some work. Besides, you can keep an eye on her better that way."

You've got no idea, thought Teddy.

Sure enough, Clancy's fears were borne out as Maureen dropped numerous hints throughout the evening that a midnight rendezvous was imminent. She even pinched his behind once behind the bar as he frantically scanned the patrons to see if anyone had noticed. To her dismay, he kept the hard-core regulars around as long as he could, even pouring a couple furtive shots on the house. She must have sensed his intent, for at midnight she unceremoniously showed them the door, calling them freeloaders and drunkards. And they left in a hurry, too, because of their fear of Brendan Cudahy.

As she locked the door, Teddy busied himself cleaning the bar and washing the heavy pint glasses. Maureen slowly pulled a chair out from one of the tables and sat herself down, staring at him, waiting him out. Teddy felt utterly humiliated. His mind raced through a series of excuses to give her for not continuing the affair, but she would not be repulsed. Finally, after twenty minutes she said, throatily, "Lover, that's a bar yer polishing, not the Queen's silver tea set. It's not getting any cleaner than that."

She rose and walked around to the back of the bar, stood behind him and rubbed his back, beginning with his shoulders. "Such tenseness," she cooed. "We've got to loosen you up." She reached around and deftly placed her hand inside his trousers. She found what she was after and softly squeezed. "There we are," she whispered.

"Not here," he said, barely under control.

She removed her hand, which was still warm, and took his. "I believe we have a reservation in the back here," she said, leading him to his room and dousing lights along the way. Once inside she was upon him like a tiger, tearing at his clothes as she searched his mouth with her piercing tongue. Unlike their lovemaking of the previous week, this was far more primitive, almost violent. Teddy allowed himself to be swept away, despising himself all the while.

After it was over, she sat astride him, breathing heavily, her long tresses a whirl of ebony encircling her shoulders and face.

"Good Lord," wheezed Clancy.

"Good Lord, indeed," she giggled. She leaned forward and placed her hands on his shoulders, pinning him to the mattress, and said the words he had come to dread: "Tell me now."

His terror at being found with her made him tear through the details at breakneck speed, her eyes widening with each new revelation. When he finished, she sat back on her haunches. It was clear that this plan went far past anything she believed her husband capable of planning out. All she could manage was, "And you think it can be done?"

"I won't know till we try it," Teddy replied truthfully.

"Sounds insane," she said, "even for him. I think he's gone round the bend, Lover."

He wished she wouldn't call him that. "Well, that's what we're goin' to do," he said defensively.

She rose and began to dress, casting a haughty look at him. "Two big time gangsters I'm mixed up with. Bloody hell." She buttoned her blouse. "Why the Book of Kells? Why not the bloody Crown Jewels?"

"I take it you feel our plan is—"

"Bloody awful. If you don't get yourselves killed, you'll surely rot in jail. The only reason a man with half a brain like yerself is going along with this is because Brendan's put the fear of God in you." She sighed deeply. "When's this disaster to occur?"

"I don't know yet. That's supposedly being determined at this moment."

She turned to go, then stopped in the doorway. "I have no choice, Ted, because I'm married to the lout. But I'm tellin' you now to get the hell out of it while you can."

"It's too late," he lamented. "I've painted meself into a corner here. It's my only way to get back to the States."

She looked at him with a mixture of disappointment and pity. "And going back there is so important to you. The bright lights, the big city." Her face softened. "Maybe you don't realize this, but in the end, you wouldn't be any the happier there. Yer one of us, Ted Clancy, a country boy from Cashel who got the taste of the high life and thinks he has to play the big man to be happy. An' what'll happen? You'll piss away any money you bring there, get in some kind of trouble like you did before, and come back to where you really belong.

"We've got our problems here, 'tis true. We're not wealthy or mannered. But me husband is only out to spite his countrymen for what happened to his father. He's a hateful man, and now I see he's lost his decency, too. The Book of Kells is somethin'…somethin' sacred. It *is* Ireland, fer Christ sake." She tossed her head back and swept the hair from her eyes, which seemed to be glistening. "Well, that's my sermon. I've got no more to say to you. Yer probably not listening, anyway."

"Maureen, I-I appreciate—"

She left only the sound of a slamming door in her wake.

Chapter Eighteen

Philadelphia

While rolling hills of Pennsylvania farmland flew by his train window, Martin readjusted the ice pack on the back of his neck and poured over the latest issue of the *Sporting News*. As of August 15 the Yankees sat atop the American League with a 79-33 record. The Red Sox, on the other hand, were woeful cellar-dwellers, and had been out of it since the second week of the season.

But the story of the year was not the Yankees and their conquest of the league. It was Babe Ruth, first, last and always. His picture was plastered all over the newspaper, and almost every column was devoted to him and his pursuit of a new home run record. Of course, he was only competing against himself, as he had set the previous standard of 59 homers six years before. He currently stood at 36 and he was mashing his way through the junior circuit. Martin fairly shivered at the thought of being on the same playing field as his idol. The prospect of facing him in a game confrontation was, well, unthinkable.

He fell asleep and had a troubling dream of home. His parents were sitting around the hearth arguing about something, probably him, and Uncle Teddy was not there at all. Where was he? Had Mike thrown him out? His parents seemed utterly miserable, and his mother appeared to have aged ten years. The train's arrival whistle awakened him, and the young man was not surprised to find his cheeks wet with tears. However, his sadness quickly turned to joy when he spied a familiar figure on the platform, saluting him grandly. It was Lefty! He scooped up his meager belongings and fairly bounded from the train.

"Put 'er there, pal!" laughed the southpaw. "I told you we'd see each other again!" The two shook hands vigorously. "Come on, we'll talk on the way to Shibe Park." Lefty hailed a cab outside the terminal and the two ballplayers climbed in. Cremins announced their destination to the hack driver and settled back. "So here you are, Clancy. Whatcha been up to since I left?"

Martin gave him a brief overview, purposely omitting Lucia and the previous evening's revels.

"Well, here's how it is with the Sox. We stink. We plain flat out stink. Not that there aren't a few good ballplayers. For instance, Slim Harriss is a pretty fair pitcher. So's Charlie Ruffing. And our centerfielder, Ira Flagstead, can really go get 'em. Billy Rogell's pretty smooth at third base, as well. But it seems like when we pitch well, we don't hit. And when we hit, the pitching falls apart. Our defense? Well, outside of Ira and Billy, we really don't have much, which really hurts the pitching staff. What's surprising is that there aren't any goof-offs on the club. But that doesn't make us any better. We just left Yankee Stadium. We were there for four days. What a fiasco! They swept all five games. They've beaten us sixteen out of twenty games so far. But what a place! Yankee Stadium's beautiful, Marty. And Ruth? It's like he's the emperor of New York. He's everything he's cracked up to be. You missed a real show."

"Where are we going after Philadelphia, Lefty?"

"Let's see…there's four games here with the Athletics. Then it's on to Washington, Chicago, St. Louis, Detroit and Cleveland. You're getting the grand tour of the American League, my friend!"

They arrived at Shibe Park just as batting practice was beginning. Bits hurriedly issued Martin a new road uniform, and the two pitchers hustled outside to join the workout. Martin spotted Carrigan, who was standing behind home plate, and jogged over. "Well, look who's back," said the manager, extending his hand.

Martin was somewhat taken back at Carrigan's appearance. He seemed worn out. The Red Sox' season had been a tough one for the proud field boss. "Hi, Skipper. I'm glad to be back. I worked hard, just like you said to. I had a really good season down at Wilkes-Barre."

"You don't have to fill me in, son. I know all about what you've been up to. I've spoken to Connick a few times, and Cremins has been hounding me about you."

"Yes, sir," he said, blushing.

"But, kid, this ain't the minors. This is the big time now. The worst guy here is as good as the best guys you faced down there. You understand?"

"Yes, Skipper."

"We brought you up because we've got a lot of games coming up, lots of doubleheaders, and we're short on arms. So learn all you can while you're with us. Who knows, you might even get a chance to pitch."

Martin was overjoyed. He took his turn throwing some batting practice, and was even greeted by Hartley and Rogell, who remembered his tryout. As fielding practice wound down, the Athletics took the field. Led by their tall, stately leader, Connie Mack, who was attired in his customary suit and high collar, the opponents scattered to their positions for warm-ups. Martin sat on the top step of the dugout and watched them. It was an all-time cast of luminaries, albeit an old one. Ty Cobb was in his 23rd season, his first with the Athletics. Eddie Collins, late of the White Sox, held down the keystone base, and old Zach Wheat joined the Georgia Peach in the outfield. The Athletics were extremely businesslike, a reflection of their manager, who sat in the dugout, fanning himself with a scorecard. Young Clancy was both happy and proud to be on the same diamond with this legend and fellow Irishman, Cornelius McGillicuddy.

The outcome of the game was predictable. The Sox lost, and neither he nor Lefty saw action. But two things made an impression on the youngster. The first was the size of the crowd. Although the game was meaningless, some 3000 fans turned out, the biggest mass of humanity that Martin had ever witnessed. The ballpark was alive with the sounds of baseball: hot dog and peanut vendors hawking their wares, the public address announcer barking lineup changes through his huge megaphone from field level, the chatter and constant stream of bench jockeying from the dugouts, the bursts of applause or crescendos of boos from the throng.

The other thing that stuck with Martin was a display of hostility so common to those who were familiar with Ty Cobb. It happened in the seventh, when the aging ex-Tiger dug in at the plate. The Sox catcher of the day, Fred Hoffman, made the mistake of riding Cobb on his so-far hitless performance. Cobb stepped backward out of the batter's box and bent over, ostensibly to rub some dirt on his hands, but really to snarl, "You'll be sorry you said that, mister." He then promptly singled, stole second, stole third, and stole home, coming in with spikes high. Hoffman, predictably, was bowled over, and Cobb was safe. He popped up, dusted himself off, shot the catcher a look of utter contempt, and strode to the Athletics' dugout amid the cheers of the crowd. His teammates, curiously, were more or less impassive. Apparently, they had seen this type of behavior too often to be fazed.

"Nasty bastard," muttered Lefty. That about summed it up.

That evening the two pitchers dined at the hotel and took a walk. Martin was amazed to find that each player was given a few dollars meal money per day. Such bigshots they were! The two were even able to take in a first-run film. Life as a major leaguer was going to be fun.

*   *   *   *

The next morning, they slept late, then took breakfast at a local eatery. A good number of the Athletics were there, but Cobb dined alone, a scowl on his face as he poured over his newspaper. The two hurlers gave a wide berth to the Georgia Peach, who ended up the berating a colored waiter because his toast was cold.

After splitting the series at two apiece, during which Cremins and Clancy took a side trip to see Freedom Hall and the Liberty Bell, the team boarded a train for Washington, DC. It was Martin's first overnight trip, and he was surprised when a red cap took his suitcase from him on the platform.

"Look nonchalant," said Lefty. "This is the Bigs, remember?"

Martin nodded, though he had no clue what "nonchalant" meant.

The Sox had chartered the last two cars on the train. This way, they could move about in relative privacy. A few beat reporters traveled with the team, but nobody talked to Martin. Except Lefty, of course. When it came time to retire for the night, the two rookies were assigned upper berths, as was the norm. They turned in quite a bit earlier than the veterans, who played cards into the wee hours.

The first day in Washington presented the Red Sox with a rainout, so Lefty took Martin on a sightseeing tour. The Irishman was quite impressed with the White House, Lincoln Memorial and Washington Monument. Of course, as he pointed out, he'd grown up in the shadow of a pretty impressive monument himself.

It should have kept on raining. The Sox were swept in doubleheaders on consecutive days.

From the Nation's Capital, the club began their Western swing. First stop: Chicago, home of the White Sox, the National League Cubs, and widespread corruption. Comiskey Park, which had been renovated and double-decked for the 1927 season, provided the Bosox' finest hour, as they took three of five from the Pale Hose. Unfortunately, all the games were close affairs, so neither Cremins nor Clancy was given a chance to pitch. Martin felt sorry for Lefty, who had been up with the big club much longer than he, but who still hadn't participated in a game. The talk of the town was not Al Capone or the latest gangland execution, but of the most recent visit by the Yanks, which saw the first home run blast over the new right field stands by their champion, Babe Ruth. Martin couldn't imagine anyone striking the ball that far, and wondered how the poor pitcher who had served it up felt.

The evening following the Sox' first game—a loss—provided perhaps the trip's most interesting moment. The Red Sox, despite their poor record, were besieged by women admirers, sometimes derisively called "Baseball Annies." For healthy, sometimes lonely men who spent much time away from home, diversions of this type were, by some players, welcomed. However, the two rookies, being relatively anonymous, were never approached, despite their youthful good looks and availability. That is, until this steamy night when the phone rang as they dressed for dinner. Martin, who loved answering the phone, was quick to pick up.

"Hello," said a husky, sensuous voice. "Is Bobby Cremins there?"

"Well," answered Clancy, "he's indisposed at the moment, miss. Whom shall I say is calling?"

"Just tell him that someone wants to meet him and that she'll be in front of the hotel in fifteen minutes."

"I'll be happy to relay the message, yes." He hung up.

"Who was that, Marty?" said Lefty, emerging from the bathroom.

"A young lady. She'd like the honor of your presence in front of the hotel in fifteen minutes. She sounds quite nice."

"Quite nice, eh? Did she tell you what she looks like, for cripessakes?"

"Uh, no, as a matter of fact."

"Well then," said the southpaw, "there's only one course of action I can take. Keep an eye on me from the window." In a flash, he had knotted his tie and was out the door.

Martin pulled a chair up to the window and got comfortable. Down below hundreds of people passed the hotel. Automobiles and elevated trains flew by. From his vantage point on the 10th floor, the people beneath him resembled ants. Everyone in America, it seemed, was hurrying somewhere. He suffered a fleeting pang of homesickness. Lefty entered his view a couple minutes later, crossing the street to a park and disappearing into the hedges that served as its outer boundary. The minutes passed, but there was no sign of the American. Martin became worried. They were, after all, in Chicago.

Almost an hour later, there was a knock on the door. Martin opened it to find his companion, a bit dirty, but obviously pleased with himself. "Cremins, what happened to you?" he said. "And how come I didn't see you come in?"

"Well," said the southpaw, flicking some grass off his lapel, "I slipped out of the hotel and bolted across the street to the park. I hid in some underbrush there and watched the hotel. And I swear, Marty, after a half-hour not *one* pretty girl appeared. Well sir, there was no way I was gonna go down there and meet an ugly girl! So I walked a block, went around to the hotel's service entrance, and snuck back up here. Ah well, it doesn't matter. There'll be plenty more opportunities for the both of us before we're through. Say, I'm hungry. Let's go eat!"

That night they feasted on steaks.

The Red Sox continued to plumb the depths of last place in St. Louis, the westernmost franchise of the American League. Clancy, who had grown up in a part of the world where the temperature rarely rose into the seventies, encountered the torrid zone of St. Louis in August. Sportsman's Park, a nondescript structure on most counts, was impressive in its ability to hold the heat, and the players soaked through their woolen uniforms minutes into their warm-ups. It got so bad that they resorted to the newest rage, placing chilled cabbage leaves under their baseball caps. Interestingly enough, this did afford some relief for an inning or so. Martin, who didn't exert any energy during the contest, still lost a couple pounds. Wilting in the heat, the Sox managed to lose four of six to the not-quite-so-lowly Browns. Then it was back to the station, another train, another series.

The ballplayers faced a maddening dilemma on the Pullman as it chugged through the blistering Midwest. If the windows were opened to allow ventilation, the cinders from the engine flew back into the passenger cars and got all over everything and in their eyes. But if they kept the windows closed, they baked. It was a good thing, then, that their cars were isolated at the rear of the train. The players spent most of their time lounging in their underwear to beat the heat.

Detroit was next. The Tigers, a respectable club, made quick work of the Sox, taking three of four at Navin Field. However, their one victory, a lopsided 11-2 thrashing, was memorable for Lefty Cremins, for he worked his first big-league inning, retiring the side in order in the eighth. Martin seemed a lot more excited about it than his buddy, who coolly said, "Nothing to it."

"Nonsense! You were masterful!"

Lefty waved him off. "Nah, Marty. I want to get in a real close one, or maybe even start a game. Then I'll be happy."

"But you struck out Harry Heilmann! He's leading the league in batting average!"

Cremins chewed on it for a few moments. "You know what, Marty? You're right. Let's go find a place that makes hot fudge sundaes."

That evening as they lay awake in the dark hotel room, Martin said, "Lefty, will Carrigan ever let me pitch?"

"Sure he will. Ya just gotta be patient, is all."

"I suppose. Hey, Bobby?" He always called Cremins "Bobby" when he was being serious.

"Yeah?"

"Would ya mind goin' to church tomorrow mornin' before we go to the ballpark? The way I figure, it couldn't hurt."

"Sure thing, Marty."

There was no act of divine intervention in Cleveland. Martin rode the bench and watched Lefty get knocked around in another mop-up role in yet another Boston defeat. The game was played before the smallest crowd they'd seen to date, only a few hundred coming out to Dunn Field to watch two clubs playing out the string.

The last night of the road trip was easily the highlight, as far as Martin was concerned. The two ballplayers, out on the town, came upon a movie theater. The featured picture was "Babe Comes Home," the film that marked the first cinematic venture of the Sultan of Swat. The movie, although entertaining, was pretty weak in the realism department. The plot revolved around the character of Babe Dugan, a slugging outfielder who is a real slob, both in his habits and appearance. He has a particular problem with his tobacco chewing, which is sloppy and unappealing to those around him. Dugan meets a charming young lady who consents to be his wife, apparently believing she can change his ways. However, for a wedding present, Dugan receives—surprise—a huge supply of tobacco. The girl pitches a fit and calls the whole thing off, which leads to Dugan falling into a terrible slump as the pennant-clinching game nears. Luckily, the girl comes to her senses, lets him have his chew, and he bashes the winning run.

The movie was pretty laughable to Lefty, but Martin was riveted by the presence of Ruth, whom he'd never seen in "action." Even in pancake makeup and grease paint, the Babe cut an imposing figure.

After a final doubleheader split with the Indians, the weary Red Sox team boarded the train for the long trip back to Boston. And it wouldn't get any easier when they got home. The Yankees would be coming to town.

Chapter Nineteen

Dublin

The courtroom was crowded, but everyone and everything seemed foreign to Teddy. Even the man sitting next to him was a stranger. No, wait a minute! He knew this guy. It was the old man with the vegetable wagon on the road to Kilkenny. "Pardon me, sir," he said, tapping the man on the shoulder. "Who is on trial here?"

The old man turned to him, the trace of a smile on his weathered face. "You've got a right nerve asking me that, son," he began, "after feeding me that fairytale about your gram and stealing me potatoes to boot, but since you're so dense, I'm happy to inform you that it's *you* who's on trial."

"All rise!" commanded the bailiff. "Court is now in session, the Honorable Justice William Stafford presiding."

Teddy felt his knees go to jelly as Vicar Stafford strode in, pausing only to cast a black scowl his way. He seated himself crisply, and Teddy tried to ease back into his chair, but found a hand firmly planted in his back. "Not you," a threatening male voice said from behind.

"Theodore Clancy," said Stafford, "you are being tried on a number of counts, ranging from conspiracy to commit robbery to adultery. How do you plead?"

Teddy was alarmed to find that he could not speak.

"All right then. Let us have the first witness."

Mike Clancy banged into the room dressed in dirty work clothes, clomped to the witness stand, and was sworn in. The whole time his eyes never left Teddy's. Mike seemed to have changed; he looked older, more

113

haggard.

"Please tell us what you know of your brother's crimes," said Stafford.

"He stole my boy," was the reply. "Spirited him away in the dead of night. Broke the mother's heart. Ruined my farm. Ruined *me*." His lower lip quivered, and Teddy cast down his eyes rather than watch his brother cry, his shoulders heaving.

"You may step down," said Stafford. "Next witness, please." Mike Clancy shuffled out, a broken man. He walked right past Martin, who seemed terribly uneasy as he took the stand. "And what has the defendant done to you, my son?" Stafford asked in his clerical manner.

"Well, sir, he, uh…well, he taught me to play baseball, you see, and he sent me off to the States, which I appreciate, but I never heard from him again. It's like he died or something. I…rather miss him terribly, is all." His voice trailed off as he lowered his head.

"Step down, my son," whispered Stafford. Martin cast a long, plaintive look at his uncle as he exited.

Teddy could guess what was coming. Molly O'Herlihy shambled into the room and took her seat on the stand, her eyes accusing, her two hulking brothers at her side. "And what crime has this regrettable man perpetrated against you, my dear girl?"

Molly, her hair wild, her face painted like a harlot's, rose from her seat and pointed at Teddy with a broken-nailed finger. "'E took my womanhood, and then my pride!" she screeched. "Promised me his love! Left me with an unborn child and ran away, he did. An' did he care that I lost the baby? No!" She turned to Stafford and a crooked smile crossed her face. "You know," she said in an odd, singsong manner, "they say I went crazy after that. That I became a wanton woman, and later on took to eating out of the garbage cans and such. I was pretty once, Your Honor." She stared at the back of her scarred and dirty hand. "My brothers come round every so often and drag me home, or to the hospital…a wonderful life, isn't it?" She turned back to Teddy. "*Isn't it!*" she screamed. Her brothers led her, shaking and sobbing, out of the courtroom.

Teddy was exhausted, but his ordeal was not over. "Last witness," called Stafford. Teddy's stomach churned as Brendan Cudahy strolled in, displaying an obvious distaste for court procedure. He plopped himself down and looked up at Stafford with an air of indifference. "Your comments on the defendant, please," said Stafford impatiently.

"Well now, and where do I begin?" he said. "Me old pal Ted. Who by the way has been stuffing me wife at every available opportunity."

Teddy squirmed in his seat as the courtroom crowd gasped.

"But still an' all, yer honor, he's still me pal. You see, we've got this caper planned...ah, 'tis a grand scheme. And we're gonna do it, by Jesus! We're gonna be rich!"

"Do go on, my son," said Stafford pleasantly.

"Do you think I'm daft?" harrumphed Cudahy. "I've said too much already. Except for one wee thing." His eyes went flat as he turned to face Teddy. "If he crosses me, I'll rip his tongue out, I will. Cut him ear to ear."

Stafford uncomfortably cleared his throat. "Er, is that all?" he said.

"'Tis enough."

"You may step down." Stafford gave a rap with his gavel to quell the murmurs of the crowd. "Well now, this calls for a verdict, I would imagine. Mr. Foreman?"

Teddy turned to the jury box to find the smiling visage of Monsignor Garvey. *Twelve Monsignor Garveys.* "Well, ah, Your Honor, we can't be too hard on the lad," the Garvey-foreman attempted. "'Tis true he's a wayward man, but he's done so much good for my church—"

"Verdict, please."

Garvey shrugged his shoulders. "Sorry, Ted me lad, but you're guilty as the day is long."

"Fine, then. Our work is done here. Take him away, now." At that, Molly's brothers moved towards him, reeking of the wharves they worked. Blood dripped from their hands.

Teddy sat up in a sweat, hyperventilating in the blackness. Knocking chairs from his path, he pawed his way to the bar and found a friendly bottle of Jamesons. "It's not real, it's not real," he chanted between shots. Gradually, he regained his composure, struggled back to his room and lay awake before muted shafts of sunlight in the bar proclaimed the dawning of another day.

*　　*　　*　　*

Still replaying remnants of the nightmare, Clancy rose and dressed, waiting around a bit for Brendan. When he failed to appear, Teddy left for St. Michan's, stopping for tea and brown bread along the way. Brendan's absence was disturbing. Coupled with Maureen's failure to bring down his lunch and that ghastly dream, he was filled with a sense of dread.

The morning's sessions went smoothly, save for one American woman who became ill when she laid eyes upon her first corpse. After bringing her upstairs to the churchyard, Teddy had returned to conclude the tour in good fashion. As he locked up for the lunch hour, Stafford approached in his customary march-step. He placed a hand on Clancy's shoulder, and Teddy nearly shook at the memory of the previous night's dream. "Have you got a minute for me, son?" he asked.

"Surely, Vicar."

"Fine, and why don't we take lunch together then, in the rectory?" The men sat down to generous bowls of steaming mutton stew and a glass of red wine. "I hear good things about you, Connor," said Stafford between bites. "It seems you've taken quite well to your duties as our sexton. You have a way of relieving the fear in these people and making them more comfortable. I believe this comes from an innate understanding and empathy for others. And, might I add, the donations in the past week have increased significantly. In a word, you've been a Godsend."

"Thank you, Vicar," he replied, trying to push away his guilt.

Stafford switched gears suddenly. "Would you consider yourself a religious person, Connor?"

Clancy chewed thoughtfully, wary of the clergyman's line of questioning. "Not as much as I should be, Vicar, though I do believe. Why do you ask?"

"Just curious. Do you have a girl?"

Maureen's face flashed before his eyes. "No, sir."

"Do you plan to marry someday?"

Teddy chuckled. "Not likely. I'm just not the type for that."

Stafford leaned forward over his stew. "You've got a way with people, son. Your devil-may-care façade belies a deeper interest and concern for your fellow man. If you don't mind my saying so, I think you'd make a fine addition to the holy order."

Teddy dropped his spoon into the thick gravy with a plunk. A smile creased his lips. "You're not serious, Vicar."

"Oh, but I am. I never joke about things of this nature." He produced a small book and slid it across the table so that it thunked against Teddy's bowl. "Read this, when you get a chance. It deals not with the Catholic priesthood, but something somewhat connected."

Teddy took the book and slipped it into his pocket, and they finished their meal in silence.

* * * *

The afternoon flew by as Teddy became more perplexed over Stafford's statements. The holy order? It was true that the good Vicar was adept at getting inside people's heads, but he was off base here. Still, Teddy found his suggestion intriguing, and decided to do a little reading that evening.

His return to the pub immediately brought him back to reality. Cudahy looked up from sprinkling some sand over the remains of a patron's lunch. "We move tonight," he cracked out the side of his mouth.

"What, so soon?"

Cudahy straightened up. "According to our man, the safe is a piece of cake. It's supposed to be cloudy tonight, with no moon. Perfect conditions."

"Are you ready for this?"

"I was born ready, boyo," he answered confidently. "I'll be needing you to meet me at the church, sometime between the hours of two and three tomorrah morning. You must make sure you're not detected. And fer Chrissake, don't forget yer key."

"How much does he want to crack the safe?"

"Don't worry yer head about that. I've got it all taken care of. Just be there when it's time."

Teddy looked past him to find Maureen standing by the bar, a plate with his dinner in her hand. Her face reflected a kind of loathing, and extreme disappointment. Had Brendan told her of the plan? It sure seemed that way. He muttered his thanks and took the food into his room, where he ate alone and read Stafford's book. The steak and kidney pie she'd prepared was tasteless to him, but he ate it anyway because he knew a long night lay ahead.

At half past eleven, Cudahy closed down the pub. He popped his head into the room and asked Teddy to clean up. "Two A.M., remember," he said. "See you at the church. Hide yourself in the graveyard and I'll find you."

"Good luck," Teddy managed.

"Candy from a babe," was the reply.

Teddy gave the bar a thorough cleaning, trying to take his mind off what was ahead. At half past one, dressed in the darkest clothes he could find, he set out for St. Michan's. The city was eerily quiet as he walked along the quay and over Ha'penny Bridge in the direction of the church. The murky sky reflected his mood. Reaching St. Michan's, he circled around to the metal doors, unsnapped the lock as quietly as possible, and waited in the shadow of a nearby copse of trees, taking an occasional pull from the flask he'd secured in his jacket. It was spooky enough being outside in the graveyard; he absolutely dreaded going down into the crypt at night.

At ten minutes to three, a small lorry pulled up to the curb across the street from St. Michan's, its headlights extinguished. A figure emerged carrying a box, and it labored around the building to the metal doors. Teddy cursed silently. The crazy bastard had done it. But where was the third man?

Cudahy gave a low whistle and Teddy emerged from hiding. "Quickly now and let's get this inside," he hissed. Teddy lifted open the doors with a minimum of squeaking. Brendan descended and Teddy followed him, easing the doors shut behind them. Once inside, he quickly fired up the electric torch he'd left on the staircase for the next morning's first tour. The two men padded down to the bottom and Brendan set the box at Teddy's feet. "Like clockwork it went," beamed Cudahy, his face purposely blackened with soot. "In and out in less than a half hour."

"And the cracksman?"

"I settled up with him after the job."

"If ya don't mind me asking, how much did he want?"

"Twenty-five hundred," Brendan answered coolly.

"You've got that kind of money?"

"I said that was how much he *wanted*. See, I made him a counter offer, you might say."

"Which was?"

"Six hundred pounds. It was all I could scrape together, I'm afraid."

"And he took that?"

Cudahy smiled. "Unfortunately, no." He pulled a wad of bills from his jacket pocket. "We had a minor disagreement in the lorry on the way here." He shrugged his shoulders innocently. "The man got greedy. Wanted more than I could pay. Started shouting at me. Even threatened to turn us in to the police. I had no choice in the matter."

Cudahy's words chilled Teddy to the bone. "What did you do to him?" he asked meekly.

Cudahy put a hand on his shoulder. "Well, ah, let's just say that where he is now, there ain't no amount of dough that's gonna help him, unless they're liquid assets." He laughed at his own joke.

"You never intended to pay him, did you?"

"Look at it this way, Teddy. The man was a fanatic for secrecy, so nobody even knew he was in Dublin. Nobody knows much about him at all, really. And why take a chance on him blackmailin' us when we strike it rich?"

Teddy had turned a ghastly white as he pressed his hand against the stone wall for support. Murder was something he was totally unprepared for.

"Don't worry, boyo. By the time they find him—if they ever find him—he'll be so bloated and chewed up by the fish they won't even know if he was a man. Now, I've got to get that lorry back before it's missed. Be careful in hiding the Book, now! It's heavy as hell, but still and all it's fragile.

"T'morrah we'll just sit back and enjoy the fireworks. Then, when the clamor for the Book reaches fever pitch, we'll make our demands known."

"If-if you say so," muttered Teddy.

Cudahy gripped him hard, much the same way he had weeks ago in the cemetery, and his eyes took on that frighteningly familiar glaze. "We're so close now. You can't fail me! I won't allow it! I'll kill you first!"

"Brendan!" Teddy stammered. "P-please calm yourself!"

Cudahy took a few hard breaths, released him, and climbed back up the stairs, slipping out into the night. Teddy, shaken, removed the stately leather-bound book from the box and sought out a seldom-visited vault. He went to a stack of caskets and creaked open the top one, revealing the corpse of a woman over two hundred years old. He could still see the blood vessels beneath the skin of her hands. Teddy placed the Book of Kells on her sunken chest and closed the lid. Making the sign of the cross, he backed out of the vault and stole up the stairs, padlocked the metal doors and fled.

Chapter Twenty

Boston

After their grueling road trip, the Red Sox were treated to a rare day off. It was a Sunday, and baseball was still banned on the Sabbath in Boston. So, Martin spent the day going to church, running errands and resting. Cremins got him settled in the Buckminster Hotel, where all the single players stayed and where the rent was only a dollar a day. It was the first time Martin ever had his own room. Lefty's was two doors down.

After breakfast, they parted ways. Martin strolled over to St. Catherine's, attended mass, and visited with Monsignor Garvey, who was delighted that the boy was back in Boston, and who encouraged him to "have faith" and not give up over his disappointment about not being used in a game as of yet. He also admonished Martin for not writing to his family. "Are ya daft, boy? Don't you think that after five months they may be wondering as to whether you're alive or dead?"

"I'll write to them today, Monsignor, and I'm sending them some money, too. You know, when I was brought up my pay went to $350 per month!" he said with pride.

"Congratulations, young man!" boomed the clergyman, as he walked him to the door. "Sendin' some cash to your family is a grand idea; they could use it. And don't forget about the church, either!"

Martin next stopped by Fenway, which stood majestic in the midmorning sunlight. And was that a touch of autumn in the air? He whistled a jaunty tune as he went through the players' entrance down to the clubhouse. Bits had already laid out his creamy white home uniform with red letters and trim for the following day's game. He sat and admired its feel and obvious upgrade in quality from the coarse hand-me-down flannels he'd worn in Wilkes-Barre. It seemed to signal that he'd truly arrived, that it was all really happening.

As he sat in front of his locker stall, feeling quite satisfied with himself, he felt a finger tap his shoulder. He turned to find a fat, florid man in a brown suit with a porkpie hat tilted back on his head. "Martin Clancy?" he inquired.

"Yessir, that's me."

The man smiled and pulled up a stool. "Bill McGuire, *Boston Globe*." The two shook hands. "I was up in Quinn's office this morning and he told me a little bit about you. Seems to me that there's a good story here. Could we chat for a while?"

The Irishman was flabbergasted. "Seriously? You want to interview me? And what for?"

McGuire let out a hearty guffaw. "Listen, kid, you may not have noticed, but we're in last place here, and have been since day one. After a while you sort of run out of things to write about. So you write about how bad the team is, but people get tired of that. So do I. Carrigan's a peach, and the team aren't bad fellows, just bad ballplayers. So then, you write about whoever's coming to town. But everybody's been through here two or three times. So I've written about Charlie Gehringer and Ty Cobb and George Sisler 'til I think I'll go crazy. And, when all else fails, you write about Ruth and the Yankees. Did you see the papers this morning? Every column, including mine, is about the Babe. People just can't seem to get enough of him. But I'm tired of it! I want something fresh, something different. Then I saw Quinn and he put me on to you." McGuire lit a fat cigar. "Bob tells me you're from Cashel. Isn't there some kind of famous castle there?"

"Yes!" replied Martin excitedly. "You've heard of it?"

"Yeah," said McGuire. "My folks are from Waterford, you know. I've never been over there myself, but someday I'll go. Anyway, how did a guy like you learn how to play baseball? And is it true that you've only been playing for a year? That's phenomenal, kid." He pulled out a pad and pencil. "Tell me your story, Clancy. From the top."

They talked for a full hour. At the end, McGuire shook his head.

"Damnedest story I've ever heard. But in this business you hear some lulus."

"Mr. McGuire," said the pitcher, "you're not having me on, are you?"

"What do you mean?"

"This will really be in the newspaper?"

"Just pick up the *Globe* tomorrow morning, kid." He patted Martin on the shoulder and waddled off.

Martin got his locker in order and walked out to the field. The morning dew had long since burned off and the empty ballpark was ghostly. He drank it in, exploring every nook and cranny of the walls, the gap down the left field line where the charred bleachers had recently been removed, and the dugouts. He saved the mound for last, pretending that he was being called in to face the Yankees. He announced himself to the "crowd": "Now pitching for Boston, Martin Clancy!" Martin strode to the hill and bent over, hands on knees, to get his sign from the catcher. He nodded, wound up and threw—*strike!* The imaginary crowd roared. Martin tipped his invisible cap to them and left the diamond.

He dined that night with Lefty at one of Boston's many waterfront restaurants. Cremins was quite impressed that Martin had been interviewed by McGuire. He chewed thoughtfully on his boiled scrod as Martin excitedly recounted the meeting. Despite the bustle of the blue-collar clientele and the noisy attention of waitresses who rushed by with foaming steins of beer, Lefty listened as if they were the last two people on earth. "Well, if that don't beat the band," said Cremins. "Here you are, still wet behind the ears, and you're getting the star treatment. I wish to hell somebody would interview me! What kind of things did you tell him?"

"Well," said Martin, remembering, "I told him about how I found out about baseball—my uncle Teddy and all—and how grand he was to teach me. And I told him about how I followed the career of Babe Ruth. We also covered my trip over here and my time in Wilkes-Barre. Of course, I told him a lot about you, too."

"How nice of you," said Lefty with mock sarcasm.

"You're not cross with me, are you, Bobby?"

"Hell no, Marty. In a way, I'm kind of happy for you. It's just that, well, you don't realize how utterly improbable your story is. If I didn't know you, cripes, I wouldn't believe it myself!" He laughed aloud. "Ah, well, it's getting late. Let's get home and get some sleep. Big series starting tomorrow."

*   *   *   *

The 1927 New York Yankees were not so much a baseball club as they were a force of nature. Their road to domination had been paved by the purchase of the club in 1915 by a couple of wealthy businessmen, James Tillinghast Huston and beer baron Col. Jacob Ruppert. These men were not afraid to spend money in improving the club, and their purchase of the young multi-talented Babe Ruth in 1920 from the financially strapped Red Sox had led to their unprecedented success in the ensuing decade. Ruth's prodigious power hitting revolutionized the game and made him a national hero. The Yankees won consecutive American League pennants in 1921 and 1922, and the World Series in 1923. By this time, they had smashed all attendance records in their cavernous ballpark, Yankee Stadium. Diminutive disciplinarian Miller Huggins, their manager, was the perfect leader for the team, despite his periodic clashes with Ruth as he attempted to rein in the boisterous superstar.

After falling short in 1924 and suffering a rare embarrassment as an also-ran in 1925 (and a horrible, injury-plagued season from the overindulgent Ruth) Huggins had infused the team with younger players and mandated that his hedonistic slugger "toe the line." Thus, they would win the AL crown again in 1926 before falling to the St. Louis Cardinals in the World Series, a tremendous turnaround that foretold a bright future.

As spring training of 1927 began, Ruth had reestablished himself as the preeminent icon of the game—and its highest paid player, at $70,000 per season. Oddly, though, baseball prognosticators were picking the Philadelphia Athletics, led by Connie Mack, to win the American League title based upon their signings of key veterans such as Ty Cobb to bolster an already solid lineup.

Led by Ruth and blossoming slugger Lou Gehrig at first base, the Yankees finished the month of April tied with the favored Athletics atop the AL standings. In May, the Ruth/Gehrig combination really got going, and the Yankees started to pull away from the A's. The infusion of youth employed by the club during their down period of the mid-decade had led to a winning blend of veterans and newcomers. Here and there, some of the other American League teams such as the Chicago White Sox made bids to knock the Yankees from their lofty perch above the standings, but every time the Pinstripers managed to beat back the threat, primarily through the bats of Ruth and Gehrig. They would finish the month 14 games over .500 and climbing, with other position players such as Bob Meusel, Tony Lazzeri and Joe Dugan contributing heavily.

June saw the Yankees finally shaking the Athletics and opening a 10 ½ game lead by its end, beginning speculation that the ballclub was perhaps the most powerful of all time. As July commenced, Ruth and Gehrig stood tied with 25 homers apiece, with three months to go. The first major threat of this month, the Washington Senators, came into a July 4 double-header with high hopes, but they were crushed in twin 12-1 defeats. Then, the Detroit Tigers had a run at them, splitting two series. But the Ruth/Gehrig onslaught continued, with Lazzeri coming on as a third weapon. The month's end would find their double-digit lead extend to 13. And though August saw the Yankee freight train slowed down a bit, none of the other teams could make a real move. Thus, as they began their September push to the pennant, the Yankees sported an astounding 17-game lead over their closest rival, Philadelphia. Ruth and Gehrig were neck and neck in the home run race, at 43 to 41, with Lazzeri third in the league at a very respectable 18.

As they arrived in Boston the first week of September, much of the speculation of baseball fans was not over whether the Yankees would take the pennant, but by how many games. They were wonderfully balanced, with their outfield of Earle Combs, Ruth and Meusel leading the way, aided by the slick-fielding, powerful infield of Gehrig, Lazzeri, shortstop Mark Koenig and third baseman Dugan, and pitchers Bob Shawkey, Waite Hoyt, Urban Shocker and Herb Pennock, to name a few. And, because of the ongoing home run derby between their preeminent power hitters, the Yanks were a tremendous drawing card on the road. Also-ran clubs such as the St. Louis Browns and Red Sox looked forward to dates with the New Yorkers as moneymakers, despite the drubbings their ballclubs would have to suffer. Thus, tickets at Fenway

Park this first week of September would be hard to come by. The whole town was buzzing with excitement.

The day the Yankee series began Cremins and Clancy took their breakfast of hotcakes and sausage in a small diner near the ballpark. They spread the sports pages of the *Boston Globe* before them. Nestled among all the anticipatory Ruth articles was the life story of Martin Clancy, complete with a Wilkes-Barre photo and minor league statistics. It was a detailed, well-written piece, and it characterized the young Irishman as a bright, highly motivated ballplayer whose sights were set on a long and distinguished Major League career. Nothing, it seemed, was left out of the article. Martin decided to enclose the clipping of his story in his letter home, which he would be mailing on the way to the park. Uncle Teddy, whose tutorial efforts were featured throughout the piece, would be especially proud. Even Lefty was in it, thank God. They were both bigshots now.

Sure enough, at the players' entrance the pair found themselves besieged by youngsters asking for autographs. Up until this day, the two pitchers had signed one here and there, but nothing like this. "Martin Clancy! There's Clancy! That must be Cremins with him!" One older lady kissed them both and said, in a heavy brogue, "The Irish of Boston are proud of ye." They made their way through the mob, signing as they went. Once inside, they caught their breath.

"Wow!" marveled Lefty. "Can you believe that?"

Martin was in a state of euphoria. "It was grand," was all he could say.

The area around Fenway Park took on a carnival atmosphere on the morning of the series opener. As noon approached, a throng of some 70,000 fans lined up outside the ballpark, hoping for admission. When they tried to force their way in to see the New Yorkers, there was a near riot. As early as 1:00 PM, ticket selling for seats stopped. After that, only standing room was available. By the time the teams began their warm-ups, people were lined around the outfield and foul lines as well, which would necessitate special ground rules. Even the buildings beyond the outfield walls had people jammed on their rooftops. Concessionaires scurried about replenishing their exhausted supplies of peanuts and candy.

The Yankees, in their road grays, took the field first, and the crowd cheered hysterically, even Monsignor Garvey and his ancient cohorts. Martin got his first look at Ruth in person, and it was a picture forever burned in his memory. The barrel chested Bambino, whose spindly legs seemed made for a much thinner man, walked purposefully to the plate for batting practice. The ball seemed to jump from his bat, with a distinct sound unmatched by his teammates, as he sent drive after drive into the delirious crowd. He clearly loved being back in Boston, where he had begun his illustrious career and was still revered. The other Yankees were no slouches, either. Gehrig, heavily muscled and grinning, followed Ruth's cannonade with some prodigious shots of his own. Then came Meusel, and Lazzeri, slugger after slugger, a monstrous display of power the likes of which was unprecedented in baseball history. Their nickname of "Murderer's Row" was no exaggeration.

The Red Sox, whose lineup in comparison packed the wallop of a popgun, took their pregame practice in a much more subdued environment. As Martin threw to his teammates, he continually looked over at Ruth, who held court in the Yankee dugout. Only the diminutive manager, Miller Huggins, paid any attention to the Sox, watching with interest as they batted and fielded. The Yankee skipper spoke with Carrigan, and the Bosox field boss seemingly winced with every word, while Huggins remained placid and confident.

The doubleheader that followed was almost anti-climactic. The clubs split the twin bill, with the home team winning in 18 innings, 12-11 and losing a five-inning game ended by darkness. Ruth, to the dismay of all, had not produced a single home run, although his tremendous swipes at the ball brought *oohs* and *ahhs* from the throng. Only first baseman Gehrig, the crown prince to Ruth, managed a circuit clout. The Babe's onslaught was temporarily stalled at 44, and what's more, the two were now tied. What a home run race this was! It was a certainty that the masses would come out again tomorrow to see this titanic contest continued.

Martin and Lefty, who spent the entire afternoon taking in the sun on the steps of the dugout, came away with a deep-seated respect of the New York ballclub. Over his dinner of pork chops and mashed potatoes Lefty said, "It's like I told you before, Marty. The same thing happened at Yankee Stadium. They're like a machine; we just got lucky in that first game today. But Ruth's mad now; Gehrig has caught him. He's a bomb waiting to explode. I just hope I'm not in there when he does."

Clancy's roast chicken fluttered in his stomach.

Lefty continued, "Now, we have an odd situation tomorrow. Because of a rainout earlier in the season, we've got another doubleheader with these guys. The thing is, we went through five pitchers today. This could be it for us—our big chance."

That night, neither hurler got much rest.

Chapter Twenty-One

Dublin

Teddy awakened from another tortured sleep to see Brendan perched atop a whiskey crate against the wall. He appeared to be in the blackest of moods. "Looka this," he grunted, tossing the morning paper onto Teddy's chest. The front page revealed no mention of the stolen Book. "Ya won't find anything inside, either."

"It's too early, Brendan," reasoned Clancy. "They probably haven't even found the empty safe yet."

"Maybe yer right, but by this afternoon the news should at least come over the radio."

"Sure it will. You're just gettin' jumpy."

"There's more. Me wife's gone."

"What do you mean, gone?"

"I mean that I woke up this mornin' and her clothes were cleaned out, along with my 600 pounds. No note, no goodbye, no nothin'. *Gone*."

"Did you tell her about last night?"

"Aye, when I got home. I was so excited I couldn't keep it in. Guess that was a mistake."

"You told her about killing the bloody cracksman, too?"

"Aye."

Teddy rolled his eyes.

"She wouldn't dare repeat a word of it," assured Cudahy. "Probably wants to get away from me, is all. Did she ever let on to you about, y'know, how she felt?"

"Me? Nah," he lied.

"Damned woman! Even I couldn't tame her." He sighed, and brightened a bit. "So, I guess it's just you and me now, pally."

"Yeah, I guess."

"Well, get yerself to work an' keep an eye on our investment. I'm gonna take a casual stroll by the college and see what's what."

A mist fell as Teddy set off for work. He wondered how the Red Sox were faring. He wondered about Maureen. He wondered about how he was going to extricate himself from the incredible mess he was in. Deftly steering the tourists away from the secret vault, he cruised through the morning, even cracking a few jokes to an especially serious group.

As the last tour made its way up the stairs and out, he found himself alone in the crypt. Normally he would be right behind them, rushing toward the fresh air. But today he found himself seeking out the casket containing the Crusader. He looked upon the body for some minutes without speaking. Finally, he said, "You might think me mad, but I envy you. You gave your life to God and country. When people come to see you they say, 'Here lies a hero.' And then there's me. Christ, what a life."

He was sitting beneath a craggy oak eating a sandwich he had purchased when he felt a shoulder tap coming from behind him. With a startled shout, he threw the food in the air and whirled around to find Maureen, her face nearly obscured by the hood of the full-length cloak she wore. "Getting a bit jumpy, are we now?" she asked.

"Don't... don't ever do that again," he rasped.

"I'll stay but a minute," she said, casting furtive glances left and right.

"Your husband isn't pleased."

"That's tough," she said tersely. "Bloody murderer, he is. Even I won't tolerate a man who sinks that low."

"And what do you think of me?"

"I don't know what to think. I'm hoping you've seen how futile this scheme is and more important, how wrong it is."

"That I have," answered Teddy, staring at the dull gray wall of the church. "It's just that I don't know how to go about ending it."

"Well, you can start by returning the damned Book! Then you turn him in!"

"It's not that easy, Maureen. If I take that course of action, I'll surely be implicated. The truth is, I haven't done anything, except of course hide the Book."

"The longer you wait, the worse it will get for you," she countered. "Besides, you have to realize unless you're a complete dolt that he doesn't plan on sharing the take on this deal. You'll end up dead like the other criminal."

Teddy exhaled deeply. "I know."

"Then what's stopping you, fer God's sake?"

Teddy couldn't answer her. A weighty moment of silence passed. "What's to become of you, Maureen?" he asked tiredly.

"Me? Well, I guess it's back to my family in Galway. I suppose they'll take me back. Of course, now I'm considered a marked woman. And I'll never stop hearin' about how everyone was correct when they said I was the right idiot for marrying Brendan. It's funny. When I told my ma she said, 'Sure and why don't you just marry the Devil?'" Her eyes misted over and Teddy wanted to look away, but his heart broke for her.

"Look," she said, pulling herself together, "I'm going to go now, and chances are I'll never see you again." She reached into the folds of her cloak, produced a roll of bills, and pressed them into his hand. "Here's half the money I pinched from him. Take it and use it to start over. You've as much right to it as me, putting up with Brendan's shit." She leaned over and kissed him lightly on the forehead. "It's time for me to go, my lover. Think well of me. I wish you luck."

Teddy watched her turn, and followed the cloaked shape all the way up King Street until she vanished in the mist.

*   *   *   *

The pub was bustling when he returned from the day's work, and Brendan was still in a foul mood. Teddy sat at the bar and Cudahy drew a pint. "No mention at all, anywhere," he spat. "I stopped a tour group leaving the college and they'd been told the book was being cleaned."

"They're waiting us out," surmised Teddy.

"Aye. But I'm not one fer waitin'," he growled.

"What are you going to do?"

"Well, I've taken the first step. This mornin' I went to a public phone on the far side of town and called in our demands."

Teddy swallowed hard. "And how much are we demanding?"

"A hundred thousand."

The number made Teddy woozy.

"I gave them until Monday to let us know if they will meet the demands. They are to lower the flag atop the post office to half-mast that morning if it's a go."

"That's only three days from now!"

"They've got the cash. Besides, a hundred thousand's a small sum to pay for a priceless treasure, ain't it?"

Teddy hated to ask the next question. "And what if they won't pay?"

Cudahy broke into his wolfish smile. "Then we'll give their beloved Book of Kells back to 'em...*one bloody page at a time*. I figure it won't take more'n one or two shredded leaves to have 'em panic."

Teddy summoned up all his courage and said, "We can't do that, Brendan. The Book's holy."

"We can, and we will, if need be. But don't worry, boyo, they'll cave in."

"You think they'll bring in Scotland Yard on this?"

"The Brits?" he snorted. "Not bloody likely. The local police'd be too proud to call them in to clean up their mess."

Teddy wasn't too sure about that.

"Which reminds me," said Cudahy, fishing around in his shirt pocket until he produced a small tan envelope. "This came for you this mornin', Western Union."

Clancy accepted the sealed envelope apprehensively.

"Well, open it, man!" barked Cudahy.

Nervously, Teddy ran his penknife along the seal. He removed the telegram and read aloud, "Greetings. Martin doing very well. Called up to Red Sox recently. God bless you. Monsignor Garvey."

"That's it?"

"Yeah, I wired him a few days ago regarding Martin's progress. It looks like he's a major leaguer."

Brendan whistled through his broken teeth. "A good omen, it is!

And we'll be there to see him play, you bet!"

Clancy managed a smile. "Sure, pally," he said, patting Cudahy on the shoulder. "If ya don't mind, I think I'll turn in. I'm feeling rather poorly."

"Sorry to hear that. Sure, go on ahead. I can handle the bar."

Teddy shouldered his way past the patrons and closed himself in his room. He sat on the bed and pulled out the telegram. He read the news about Martin once again, a flush of pride coming over him. But this surge of emotion quickly turned to abject sadness, and tears rolled down his cheeks as he read the second part of the note: DO NOT RETURN. UNSAFE HERE. M. OHERLIHYS BROTHERS FOLLOWING ME TO FIND YOU. DIRE CONSEQUENCES IF YOU ARE CAUGHT. SORRY.

"So that's it, then," he said to no one in particular. Everything for the past few days had pointed to his bailing out. His horrible dream, Stafford's talk, the murder, Maureen. And now this. That he was through with Cudahy was certain; now he had to figure a way to resolve the mess before Monday without having the manuscript destroyed or himself rubbed out. As he lay awake listening to the revelry of the drinking crowd, a plan began to take shape in his head. By the next morning, he'd decided on a course of action that he prayed would save the day—and maybe his soul.

Chapter Twenty-Two

Boston

September 6 dawned, ominously cloudy with a slight chill. Martin had watched the sky lighten as he lay awake in bed. He'd managed some fitful snatches of sleep, but that was all. He donned a bathrobe and padded down the hall to Lefty's room, but there was no response to his knock. Perhaps Lefty had gone out for an early walk, which wasn't uncommon. Little did he know that Cremins had only fallen asleep at 4 AM himself, and was dead to the world.

The Irishman returned to his room and washed up, putting on his freshly laundered shirt and a blue tie. He was increasingly hungry, and resigned himself to a breakfast alone. Martin was reaching for his hat when there was a knock at the door. "Be right there!" he sang out, checking himself in the mirror. Indeed, he looked and felt just grand. Martin was happy Lefty had come around.

He opened the door and his jaw went slack. There before him stood George Herman Ruth, in a camel's hair coat and matching cap, a cigar protruding from the side of his mouth. "Hiya, kid!" he bellowed. "Are you this Clancy character I've been reading about?"

Martin struggled to get his mind into gear. "Why y-yes, Mr. Ruth. Martin Clancy, that's me."

"That's great. Say, kid, I read about you in the papers. I said, 'I've gotta meet this kid!' How about joining me for breakfast? I know a great place a block from here where we can have some privacy."

"That'd be grand," the young pitcher managed. And so, Martin Clancy and his idol went to breakfast.

Luckily, for the Babe it was still pretty early, and the pair only had to stop four or five times for autographs along the way. Ruth was absolutely charming to the fans, especially the children, making sure they got Martin's autograph also. "My pal here is a famous baseball player too, y'know," he'd say each time. The young ballplayer felt like a million dollars.

They were given a back table in the fancy Rochambeau Hotel's restaurant. The walls were adorned with ornate red and gold tapestries, and heavy draperies muted the otherwise brilliant light generated by numerous crystal chandeliers. There was an air of Victorian elegance about the place, and Martin thought it was odd that breakfast, which he associated with cold morning dampness and the smell of the barnyard, could be taken in such lavish surroundings. But then, he was dining with a king. A waitress came over, fairly gushing, and Ruth jovially flirted with her. He was in high spirits this day. "Let's see now," he began, his eyes never crossing the menu, "I'd like three eggs...no, make that four, scrambled...a steak, medium rare...some fried potatoes...onions on the steak, don't forget...toast...and a pot of coffee." He pulled her close and added, "With a shot of Irish in it, if you don't mind." He looked at his companion. "How about you, kid?"

Martin was almost too amazed to order. "Two eggs, scrambled, and tea, please."

Ruth raised his eyebrows. "That's *all?* Hell, kid, you'll never be a real major leaguer eating like that." He turned to the amused waitress. "Honey, add a stack of hotcakes to his order. Come to think of it, I'll take a stack myself." The waitress happily retreated, mentally calculating the tip she would receive from such a spread. The Babe lit a cigar and blew out a cloud of blue smoke. "Now let me get this straight, kid," he began while tucking a napkin under his broad chin. "You left your family to come here and play ball because you read about me?"

"Something like that, er, Babe. I guess, in a way, you inspired me to try."

"You miss your family, kid?"

"At times I do. I miss them terribly at night sometimes, when I have time to think. I want to make them proud of me. I would imagine that yours are proud of you."

135

"Both dead," he said, curtly. "They didn't take a great interest in me, sorry to say."

Martin could've kicked himself. Of course! Ruth had spent his childhood in reform school. How could he have been so stupid? "Well, Babe," he said, "from what I can see, there's a great many people in this country who admire you, and that's a fact. Especially children. Oh, how their faces light up when they're around you!"

The food arrived on China plates with silver domed covers, which the waitress deftly removed. The slugger dug in. Between chews he said, "Kid, in this game—if you stay in it long enough—you're gonna meet all kinds. Some people are great. Others just want to fleece you. And the women can be a pain in the ass if you don't know how to pick 'em. But the kids are all right. They don't try to lie to you or cheat you. They tell you exactly what's on their mind. That's why I get along with 'em. There's no bullshit. Make sure you be nice to kids. I may do a lot of…ah…unsavory things, but around kids, I'm on my best behavior. Because I know what it's like for somebody to take an interest in a lonely kid. That's what happened to me in the school I went to. There was this guy named Brother Mathias…a big, strong man...and at first, I was really frightened of him. But then, I don't know, he saw something in me that others didn't. Taught me how to play baseball, showed me something I could be good at. And I never forgot it. If I can have a good effect on a youngster, well, I can't take a chance on letting him down."

"Is that why you've taken an interest in me?" said Martin, trying hard to make a dent in his mountain of food.

Ruth paused and looked him in the eye. A smile creased his broad face. "Yeah, something like that," he replied, and tore into his pancakes. From there the conversation went in all directions, and Martin could see that before him sat a microcosm of the game—indeed, of the country—he had decided to embrace: brash, powerful, rough, imbued with old-fashioned values but looking forward to a limitless future. The Babe was all he could ever be in Martin's eyes. He had fit the bill as hero and idol, with lots to spare. Martin was proud to be his countryman.

The Babe picked up the tab and tipped the grateful waitress twenty dollars, peeling the bills off a wad as big as his fist. The two ballplayers shook hands and parted company at the door of the Rochambeau. "Well,

136

kid," said the Yankee star, "I guess I'll see you at the ballpark later. Looks like a great day for a game, but tell your team to watch out. I feel lucky today."

He gave a wink and then, suddenly, he was gone, leaving Martin to wonder if it had all been a dream.

Chapter Twenty-Three

Dublin

On Friday, Teddy marched through the sunshine along the Liffey, a man on a mission. He ran through the morning's paces smartly, then at lunchtime headed to the General Post Office—where the flag of the Irish Republic flew at full staff—and mailed a letter. On his way back to St. Michan's he purchased a burlap sack the size of a pillowcase. After the afternoon's final tour was concluded he sought the secret casket and lifted the lid. The woman inside, who still sported a mane of white hair, seemed to be smiling at him. "Thanks fer watching me book, mum," he whispered as he gently removed the heavy volume and placed it in the sack. Returning it to her chest, he eased the lid shut again. "Sleep well, mum," he said as he flicked off the central light switch that helped illuminate the main passageway.

That night he spent a lot of time at the bar, in front and behind, observing closely the movements of Brendan Cudahy. The tavern keeper seemed on edge, but supremely confident that the college authorities would accede to his wishes. Cudahy was even proud of his choice of the General Post Office as the signal station for the authorities. It had been the rebels' headquarters in the 1916 Rising, and it was regarded as a symbol of the heroic stand made by the doomed Citizen Army. Now he was using it to slap the face of the government that had betrayed his father, and he thought that was rather fitting. By mid-evening, Brendan was well into his cups and retired to a table to play cards and drink with his cronies. Meanwhile, Teddy worked the bar and mentally mapped out phase two of his plan.

Saturday dawned, dreary and unusually cool for this time of year. Teddy rose early and went east, following Aston Quay to Burgh Quay, George's Quay, City Quay and beyond until he reached Dublin Harbor. Within an hour, he had completed his business there and hurried back along the gurgling Liffey, its peat-stained waters dark and malevolent. He barely made it back to St. Michan's for the first tour. Lunchtime was spent finishing Vicar Stafford's book which, to say the least, had been enlightening.

As if by some strange coincidence, there were no people lined up for the afternoon tours, and it had begun to rain, so Teddy retired to the crypt. It was odd how he'd become accustomed to the surroundings, and no longer resorted to strong doses of liquor to calm his nerves. In fact, he felt somewhat safe now. *Dead people can't hurt you*, he reasoned, *only the live ones, like Brendan Cudahy.* Pulling up the special coffin's lid once more, he removed the burlap-encased Book of Kells and sat down on a dusty coffin. Teddy drew his hand torch close, having decided not to use the central lighting system. He wanted to be alone. Strange, but outside of the day he had first viewed the Book of Kells with the American collegians he'd pretty much let it alone, almost afraid to trespass. Now it was his for the afternoon.

Slowly, reverently, he turned page after page, marveling at the elaborate, whimsical extravagance of Celtic art. Saints, angels and other characters danced along the margins of the wonderfully transcribed calligraphy. This was the history of his country, the glorious struggle of his God-fearing ancestors who had forged the strength of the Irish people. He drew courage from the Gospel and vowed not to let harm come to this treasure.

*   *   *   *

Saturday night was a wild one at Cudahy's Pub. Three separate scuffles erupted that Brendan and Teddy had to break up. In each case, the offenders were shown the street, but Teddy had his shirt torn to shreds in the final bout between two sodden docksmen. "Oh, to be done of this place," he whispered to himself as he cleaned a gash over his eye before falling into bed.

Sunday he slept later than normal, then dressed in his finest clothes and strolled over to St. Michan's to attend mass. The fact that it was Anglican mattered not a bit to him. The noon service would be the last, and Vicar Stafford was presiding. Teddy sat in the first pew and Stafford even smiled at him once, happy to see his sexton observing the Sabbath. Afterward, Stafford warmly greeted Teddy out front as the parishioners exchanged pleasantries and milled about. "Well, it's surely a surprise to see young Connor at my service this fine morning. And what brings you out this lovely day?"

"Vicar, it's important that I speak to you," said Teddy quietly.

Stafford's eyebrows knit at his youthful friend's discomfort. He put his willowy arm around Teddy's shoulders. "Let's talk in my office, son."

Once they were seated in the dark wood-paneled room, which was lined with bookcases filled with theological treatises, Stafford settled back in a leather chair and tented his fingertips. "You're troubled," he said with concern.

"Deeply."

"And you think I can be of help?"

"I truly hope so." He shifted uncomfortably. "It's a long story, I'm afraid."

"Connor," he answered, "you've nothing to fear. Say what you have to say."

"Well, Vicar, for starters, my name's not Connor O'Shea." Beginning with his arrival in Dublin, Teddy replayed the whole story, leaving nothing out, even his affair with Maureen. Stafford listened impassively, never changing his facial expression or position. Teddy could get no read at all as to what he was thinking. After more than an hour of painful confession, he slumped back into his chair, exhausted. "That's the lot of it, Vicar," he concluded, "and I hope you don't hate me already."

Stafford paused, rubbed his eyes and sat back, staring at the wooden-beamed ceiling. Teddy waited on edge for his reaction. Finally, the clergyman cleared his throat. "So, as I understand it, we are at this moment sitting over the Book of Kells, which is concealed in the crypt below."

"That's right."

"And which will be destroyed piece by piece starting tomorrow if the ransom is not agreed to."

"Yes."

"Mother of God," sighed Stafford, shaking his head slowly. "Do you see now what happens when we live too much in the material world, Ted?"

"I do, Vicar."

Stafford straightened up in his chair and looked Teddy squarely in the eye. "This man must be brought to justice," he said solemnly. "Excuse me while I make a call. Don't be alarmed; I'll not hint at your identity or the situation as I know it to be."

Teddy squirmed as the clergyman left. The minutes crept by slowly. When Stafford returned he leaned back in his desk chair and folded his arms across his chest. "I just spoke with a friend of mine who works at Trinity College. In a roundabout way, I got him to corroborate what you've said. What I wanted to ascertain is just whom we're dealing with. It seems the Yard has been summoned to assist the locals, but they have few clues. Your thief was very thorough."

"And now, very dead," added Teddy.

"Yes, quite. Well, Ted Clancy, what do you want to do?"

"I have a plan, Vicar, but I'll need your help. I think I can bring Brendan out for capture and still preserve the Book. But you see, ah…"

"Your plan does not allow for you to be captured also, is that it?"

"Yes."

Stafford took a deep breath and then blew it out. "Ted, you've shown great courage and wisdom in coming to me. As far as I can see, you are no criminal. You've done nothing terribly wrong. In fact, I'd consider you somewhat heroic for trying to spare this holy relic from destruction. I think there is no further penance you have to serve than the pain of your confession."

"Then you'll help me?"

"You'll not walk alone, my son," he promised.

Chapter Twenty-Four

Boston

Despite slow moving, foreboding clouds that hung overhead, the crowds by noon were returning to Fenway, massing for another assault on the ticket windows. Again, the two young pitchers had to pick their way through a horde of admirers and well-wishers. Once inside, the clubhouse took on a fatalistic atmosphere. Tony Welzer was tabbed as the first game's starting pitcher, and no one envied his position. In fact, it seemed that the other ballplayers steered clear of him. Only Hartley, who would be catching him this day, put a fatherly arm around him and offered some words of reassurance. Then Welzer, who must have found the room suffocating, left for the playing field. As soon as he was out of earshot Hartley cracked, "Stay loose, you pitchers." There were a few forced guffaws, but it was strictly gallows humor.

By warm-up time, the throng was again reaching unmanageable proportions. Lefty was extremely impressive as he warmed up on the side during batting practice. "I've really got it today," he remarked to Clancy at the end of his workout. "Let them bring on that big baboon, I'm ready for him." Martin marveled at his friend's bravado, for even as he spoke, the Yankee hitters were launching practice homers into the deepest recesses of the ballpark.

From the very beginning of the game, it was obvious that Welzer was not at his best. The visitors fairly toyed with the right-hander. Boston's outfield troika of Shaner, Flagstead and Tobin were run ragged, and Phil Regan at second base nearly had his head taken off by a Gehrig line drive in the first inning.

142

By the fifth frame, it was 6-0 Yankees and the handwriting was on the wall. Carrigan, who'd spent the game on the top step of the dugout tossing pebbles to and fro, shook his head in frustration. "All right," he said finally, "I need someone to get loose. Does anyone think they can get these guys out?" There was a momentary silence as the players studied their shoelaces.

"Hell," said Cremins, rising, "I can get 'em out!"

"Fine, go warm up," said the harried manager. Then, almost as an afterthought he added, "Clancy, why don't you keep him company?"

Martin grabbed his glove and scurried up the steps to join Lefty on the sideline for warm-ups. Scattered raindrops punctuated the sense of immediacy, and they began throwing hurriedly, purposefully. Backup catchers Hoffman and Bill Moore were dispatched to assist them. In the stands, spectators could hear the pop-pop of fastballs striking leather. After twenty or so pitches, they both were ready. Then they could do nothing but stand, watch, and wait.

Welzer faced the Babe with a man on and got behind in the count. With the menacing Gehrig awaiting his turn, the pitcher decided to challenge Ruth, with disastrous results. The Bambino poled a long blast into the right-field bleachers and cruised around the bases with his patented home run trot as the Fenway faithful went berserk. Welzer stared at the sky, an abject figure of defeat. As Ruth crossed the plate, Carrigan was already on his way out to the mound. The field boss and pitcher conversed, with Hartley an interested bystander. To everyone's amazement, Carrigan left him in. The crowd booed lustily.

"How do ya like this," muttered Lefty, and the two dejected hurlers returned to the dugout.

Carrigan must have known something, however, because the weary hurler was able to summon whatever he had left and work his way out of the inning, inducing Gehrig to foul out to the catcher and Joe Dugan to bounce into a twin killing, erasing Meusel, who'd singled. Upon his return to the dugout, Welzer approached his manager. "Skipper, I'm spent," he said.

"That's all right, Tony," replied Carrigan. "You did your best. Thanks for finishing out the inning. Clancy, you start the seventh."

Lefty, who had been halfway out of his seat, sat back down and looked at his friend. "So I guess it's you," he remarked. "Knock 'em dead, Marty." He was barely able to mask his annoyance.

While the Sox batted, Clancy scaled the steps of the dugout and began throwing again. There was a mild ripple of applause from the stands near the dugout, but Martin barely acknowledged it, blocking everything out but Moore, who was catching him. He hoped Lefty wasn't mad at him for being chosen.

Back in the dugout, Carrigan slid over to the perturbed Cremins and whispered, "We're almost out of pitchers and we have a game left today with these guys. I figure this game's out of reach and I don't want to waste you if I don't have to. So, I'm giving the kid a chance."

"Sure thing, Skip," said Lefty. "But cripes, what a spot!"

"Well, he's gotta learn some time," said the manager.

The Red Sox batters went quietly in the bottom of the sixth, so Clancy only threw a few practice pitches. No matter. He was ready. As the Yankees flipped their gloves to the ground and headed for their dugout, Martin jogged to the mound. The public address announcer rose from his seat near the Sox dugout and went to the home plate area where he raised his huge megaphone and cried, "Now pitching for Boston, Martin Clancy!"

There was a smattering of applause, probably from Garvey's section. Then some leather lung behind the plate loudly observed, "Another lamb for sacrifice!" This brought raucous laughter from the crowd.

Hartley caught Martin's eight warm-up pitches, all fastballs, then threw down to second base. He chugged out towards the mound, where Martin met him halfway. "All right now, Clancy, same signals as always. Fastball, one. Curve, two. And three for that bastard pitch of yours, but I hope I don't have the call for it." He spat, slapped his battery mate on the rump, and returned to his position.

The pitcher walked to the back of the mound to collect his thoughts. The clouds had gotten thicker now, and Martin, ever the Irishman, could smell a heavy rain coming. Most of the spectators, who had again seeped onto the playing field, wore jackets and fedoras, which had replaced the straw hats of summer. He rubbed up the baseball, turned, and stepped to the pitching rubber.

Mark Koenig, the Yankee shortstop, dug in and cocked his bat. Clancy bent over and peered in at Hartley for the sign. Fastball. Martin nodded, kicked and dealt. "Stee-rike!" shrilled the ump. Martin allowed himself the faintest of grins as he received Hartley's return throw.

Koenig nodded to himself, revealing he'd just wanted to see the rookie's stuff. Now he was ready. Hartley again signaled fastball. Ssschup! Strike two. Koenig frowned, obviously perturbed that he'd swung way too late. Now that he had him set up, Hartley signaled for a curve. Predictably, Koenig couldn't pull the trigger. He took strike three looking, shouldered his lumber and shuffled back to the dugout amid the hoots of the Bostonians.

Next up was Benny Bengough, the catcher. He fared little better than Koenig, managing to foul off a couple of pitches before going down on a 2-2 fastball.

Now the Red Sox bench came alive. "Way to go, Marty!" called out Lefty from the dugout steps.

The Yankees likewise started chirping in their dugout. "Hey Busher!" yelled one of them. "Keep throwin' that shit and see what happens!" A litany of various and sundry insults followed until the New York bench became a cacophony of derision.

Martin smiled inwardly. He felt in complete command, and the pitcher Pennock was due up. Hartley called for fastballs and Clancy quickly got ahead, 0-2. Much of the crowd was on its feet now, clamoring for the Irishman to strike out the side. Hartley put down the number one. Martin reared back and fired. Pennock, grossly overmatched, closed his eyes and swung mightily. Had the arc of his bat been a centimeter higher, he would have swung over the ball completely. As it was, by the tiniest of margins he grazed the top of the ball, which dribbled harmlessly toward the pitcher's mound. Pennock set sail for first, his feet churning. Martin, whose textbook follow-through left him in perfect position to field the ball, pounced on it. He picked it cleanly and soft-tossed it on a straight line for first baseman Phil Todt's nose. He then began walking towards the dugout and was almost to the foul line when Todt dropped the ball and Pennock safely crossed the bag.

The crowd booed poor Todt, who embarrassedly stabbed at the ball with his hand as if he wanted to crush it. Then, gloving it, he walked to the mound, meeting his pitcher on the way. "Sorry," he said, dropping it into Clancy's glove.

Martin could not have cared less. This was but a temporary setback, and the crowd was now behind him. He reminded himself that he'd now have to pitch from the stretch position and keep Pennock close to first, not that the pitcher would try to steal in a blowout situation like this. He looked in at Hartley as the New York leadoff batter, Earle Combs, set himself. Grover signaled for a curveball, which was a good strategy; everyone else had been started with a fastball. Martin ground the ball into his hip and glanced over his left shoulder at Pennock, who was hugging the base as he'd expected. He brought his hands to eye level then settled them at his chest. He exploded from this position and drove to the plate.

"Ball!" said the umpire.

Clancy winced. It didn't look like a ball to him. A tad outside perhaps, but that was splitting hairs. Hartley called for a fastball. Martin went through his motions and delivered.

"Ball-high!"

Clancy snapped at Hartley's return toss with his glove. What was the umpire trying to do to him? That pitch cut the plate! Hartley called for a curve. Martin delivered, this time so far inside that the catcher had to scramble in the dirt for it.

"Ball three!"

Combs, the finest leadoff hitter in the game, smiled at the young pitcher. He was way ahead and had gotten the benefit of the doubt on two close pitches. He guessed fastball. He guessed right. Martin's offering was rifled back past his ear and into center where Flagstead made an aggressive scoop and throw to hold Pennock on second.

Hartley, standing at the plate, gave Martin the palms-down "stay calm" signal. The rookie gave a weak wave to signify that he understood. But inside he was burning. If only Todt had caught his throw, he wouldn't be in this mess! As the next batter, Tony Lazzeri, approached the plate, Martin could see out the corner of his eye a large, gray shape making its way to the on-deck circle, a load of bats on its shoulder.

"Get this guy, Marty!" yelled a friendly voice from the Bosox' dugout. The crowd was getting progressively more restless.

"I'm in control, I'm in control," the young right-hander repeated to himself. Then he walked "Poosh-em-up Tony" on five pitches. Bases loaded.

"Time!" yelled Grover Hartley. The catcher flipped back his mask and proceeded to the mound, stealing a glance at his manager in the dugout. Ruth remained in the on-deck area and, although the crowd noise was rising steadily, sensing the moment, Martin was sure he could hear the grinding sound of the slugger twisting the bat handle in his enormous hands. By the time Hartley got there, the rookie appeared to be in a trance. "Clancy! Snap out of it!" he growled. Martin was jolted out of his funk. "Listen to me," he continued. "You got bases full, two out. We got nowhere to put this guy. Besides, Gehrig's up next. You've gotta bear down, kid, or Carrigan will yank you outta here so fast your head'll spin. Go to your full windup. I'm calling fastball first pitch. Let's go get 'im!" He turned on his heel and hustled back to the plate.

"Oh ho ho! Well, what have we here!" bellowed Ruth as he stepped in. "My old pal! How goes it, kid?" Hartley put his head down, and even the umpire appeared to be smiling. Martin was not. Everything was out the window now. This was war. "Let's see what ya got!" Ruth said, rocking back into his batting stance. The crowd was stamping its feet and whistling.

Martin pumped, kicked, and unloaded a simply pathetic fastball, which bounced six inches in front of the plate. Hartley, who had to smother the ball, was nearly decapitated by the Bambino, who swung so hard at the meatball that he almost corkscrewed himself into the ground. The catcher, on all fours, looked up and hissed, "I called for a fastball!"

"That *was* my fastball," replied the pitcher, his voice trailing off.

"Gimme another one of those fucking balloons, kid!" laughed Ruth with glee. "I won't miss it this time. Honest!"

Hartley called for another fastball, and this one was much better; in fact, it was the best fastball Martin threw all day. To the average human, even an experienced ballplayer, it would have been nothing more than a blur. But Babe Ruth was the quintessential fastball hitter at the height of his powers, and he somehow managed to be out in front of the pitch, smoking it foul into the Red Sox dugout and scattering Martin's teammates, who waved white towels of surrender. The young pitcher's heart sank when his hero roared, "Come on, kid, throw me a *real* fastball!" The crowd, feasting on the antics of their prodigal son, howled like lunatics. Martin was suddenly filled with an overwhelming urge to plant a fastball in his idol's earhole.

Hartley, in his catcher's squat, had an idea. He squinted up at the slugger and cracked, "All right, ya big monkey, ya want a fastball? Here it comes!" He then put down three fingers for the fadeaway.

Martin nodded with relief. Of course! The fadeaway! Inside his glove, he positioned his fingers on the ball exactly as Uncle Teddy had shown him, laying his index and middle fingers across the laces and digging in his fingernails. *Now you'll get yours*, he thought. Then he double-pumped, kicked and heaved.

POW! Martin nearly got whiplash as he tried to find the ball, which whistled over his head. "Holy SHIT!" shouted second baseman Regan, looking straight up and then bending over backward as the ball climbed at a steep angle. Flagstead in center field never even moved. In fact, the entire ballpark stopped for a few heart-pumping moments to track the flight of the missile. Even the Babe froze to admire the grandeur of the clout. It just kept rising and rising, clearing the 35-foot high board fence in dead center field and sailing out of sight.

Newspaper accounts the following day would describe this shot as Ruth's longest drive ever, even longer than his legendary poke in Tampa against the Giants in 1919 when he was a Red Sox. The homer in Comiskey Park earlier this same season paled in comparison, they marveled. Some estimated the ball had traveled 500 feet.

Martin stood stock still on his mound of misery, chin on his chest, as Ruth made a grand tour of the basepaths. He waved his cap to the adoring crowd and let their cheers wash over him. As he rounded third he turned to Martin and yelled, "Better luck next time, kid!" He crossed the plate and was enveloped in the raucous Yankee dugout amid much backslapping and glad-handing. Martin was so wrapped up in this performance that he hardly noticed Carrigan and Hartley standing next to him.

"Not your day, son," said Carrigan, the understatement of the year. "I'm gonna bring in Cremins to relieve you." He motioned with his left hand and Lefty began to walk in from the warm-up area near the first base stands. Martin hadn't even noticed Lefty was again throwing.

"This is what I want you to do, son," said the manager. "Get inside, take a shower and go home. The way this is looking, we may be here a while longer. So do what I say and we'll get after it again tomorrow." Martin accepted a pat on the backside and trudged toward the dugout, leaving manager and catcher alone. "I hated taking him out," he heard Carrigan say. "I did it for his own good."

Hartley nodded and spat. "Hey Bill," he said, "think that ball came down yet?"

As Martin crossed the foul line, his friend intercepted him. "I'm sorry, Marty," was all Lefty could manage.

"Just get them out, Bobby," was the reply. Then he tipped his cap to the crowd and disappeared beneath the stands.

Chapter Twenty-Five

Dublin

"Today's the day, boyo," said Brendan optimistically as they shared a pot of tea in Cudahy's apartment above the pub. Since Maureen's departure, the rooms had gone to seed and the dining table was strewn with days-old newspapers that Brendan had searched in vain for news of the stolen Book. Trinity College had also maintained its story of the volume being cleaned, so that the population of Ireland, save for a few school officials, the police, and—unbeknownst to Cudahy—Scotland Yard, was completely in the dark as to the plight of their most treasured manuscript.

"During your lunch break take a stroll by the General Post Office and check the flag," said Cudahy. "If it's at full staff I want you to bring the first page with you from work this afternoon, and I'll take over from there. Any questions?" It was clear he did not expect any.

"No. Just a minor problem," replied Teddy tentatively.

Cudahy frowned. "What problem? Yer not chickening out, are you?"

"No, no, nothing like that," assured Teddy with his most winning smile. "It's just that tonight the good Vicar wants me to hang about till seven to help the custodian clean the pipes of that damned big organ we've got. Seems it's a bit too tarnished for the boss's liking."

"Self-important fool," Cudahy sneered. "Still, you have to do it, I suppose. And it won't affect a thing, because they're not gonna get the scraps till I drop 'em off tomorrah. That is, of course, if any of this is necessary. I still say they're gonna give in. You'll see."

"And if perchance they decide not to, then you can expect me, page in hand, by half past seven," promised Clancy.

"Then it's all set."

Clancy rose to go, and Brendan extended his hand, which enveloped Teddy's in a bone-crushing grip. "Don't fail me," he warned, his eyes blazing under beetled brows.

"It's a cinch, pally," were Teddy's last words as he clacked off down the staircase and into the teeming street.

Monday morning's tours went slowly and Teddy, usually the affable, wisecracking host, was understandably a bit curt while answering questions he had fielded charmingly, day in and day out. At lunchtime he half-walked, half-ran up Henry Street to the General Post Office, knowing somehow the outcome of the visit. Sure enough, the flag of the Republic of Ireland flew proudly at full staff, flapping the gentle summer breeze.

At the conclusion of the last afternoon session, Teddy reported to Stafford's office, where he found the grim clergyman waiting for him. "All right, son," he said, rubbing his temples, "what do we do next?"

"For now, we wait. I expect that at seven-thirty he'll come looking for me. I'd estimate he'll make it here by a quarter to eight. So, I'll need you to bring up the police at seven o'clock. Tell them you received an anonymous tip as to the Book's whereabouts and that the thief will be coming to claim it within the hour. Tell them to hide in the churchyard and let him enter the crypt, which I shall leave unlocked. Then they will have him red-handed with no way of escape."

"And you will be—"

"Long gone."

"Where will you go to, son?"

"Not to worry, Vicar, I've made provisions. However, it's not likely you'll see me again." Teddy felt genuinely sorry about this, for he had developed and admiration for the fatherly cleric.

Stafford checked his watch. "It's only half past six. Come with me to the church and we'll pray for guidance."

The two men spent the next half-hour in deep prayer, the Vicar hoping that God agreed he was doing the right thing, Teddy hoping that Cudahy would react true to form and show up in a rage to exact punishment upon his cowardly partner.

At two minutes to seven Stafford rose and placed his hand on the shoulder of the still-kneeling Teddy. "This is it, then," he said sadly.

"Yes, Vicar. Now, I'm going to go quick downstairs and remove the Book from the coffin while you make your call. I'll place it back on top of the casket. That would be the vault three on the left side as you enter. The Donaghy family."

"Right. I'm off to the phone."

As Stafford hurried away, Teddy padded outside to the metal doors and unfastened the lock. He slipped downstairs and removed the Book of Kells for the last time, placing the burlap-closed package upon old Mary Donaghy's oaken coffin. Retreating to the main passageway, he took one last look at the strange place in which he had spent the past tumultuous weeks, where he'd come to know every vault, every inhabitant, as though they were family. Snapping off the main switch, he hefted the electric torch and started for the stairs. He had reached the landing when Stafford began descending toward him, his face an ashen mask. Brendan Cudahy followed close behind, a revolver at the Vicar's ear.

"This is madness, Brendan," pleaded Stafford.

"Shut up and keep moving!" he barked, pushing the clergyman ahead of him. When Cudahy's eyes fell upon Teddy, he nearly turned purple with rage. "Bloody liar! Try to cheat me, will you?" He pushed the cleric forward so that his two enemies stood together before him.

Teddy did not know if Stafford had had the chance to make his call, but figured he must try to delay their deaths in any event. "H-how did you know?" he managed, his pulse pounding in his ears.

"Well," said Cudahy, "it all started with this." Teddy's heart sank as the criminal produced the telegram from Monsignor Garvey. "Fell out of yer shirt during the brawl at the pub the other night. I figured there was no way you were going back to Boston now. I had the feeling you'd lose your nerve, not that you ever had any, you lying worm."

Teddy began to sweat. He must keep Cudahy talking. "Pally," he tried, "you've got this all wrong—"

"Don't insult me intelligence!" bellowed Cudahy. "I trusted you, an' now look! You were probably screwin' me wife, too!" The hand holding the pointed pistol began to shake violently.

"Brendan, think of what you're doing," reasoned Stafford, somehow maintaining his sense of calm.

"I have thought about this!" he screamed. "I've planned it all out! Perfectly! And I'll not be denied what's mine, Goddamn it!"

The words had barely escaped his mouth when Teddy flung the electric torch wildly, striking Cudahy a glancing blow as it whizzed by his ear. Reflexively he fired twice as the torch smashed into the wall and plunged the crypt into inky blackness. Teddy dove to the floor and scuttled down the corridor, hearing the groans of Stafford, who'd apparently been wounded. *Please don't let him die, Lord,* he thought as his eyes began to adjust to the dark. According to his calculations, he was in front of vault three, right side. The Crusader's vault. Summoning his courage, he crawled across the passageway to three-left, snatched the sack, felt for a space between two stacks of coffins and wedged himself in, bringing his breathing under control. *Don't panic, don't panic* he thought to himself as he clutched the bulky burlap bag to his chest.

"Come out, ya bloody coward!" screamed Cudahy, crashing into coffins as he wandered aimlessly. Thank God he didn't know where the central light switch was. But Teddy realized he couldn't sit still. If the police didn't arrive, it would only be a matter of time until Brendan found his bearings and hunted him down like a rat. He had to force the issue.

Suddenly there was a scream and a shot rang out. Teddy nearly cried out himself but quickly surmised that Cudahy must have backed into a corpse. He was down to three bullets. Shuffling sounds came from vault one-right. Time was running out.

A coffin lid crashed closed. Cudahy had progressed to two-right. Teddy moved to the portal of his vault and assumed a crouching position, the Book slung over his right shoulder. When Brendan's silhouette filled the passageway, he sprang into action, bull-rushing his pursuer and ramming him with his free shoulder. Cudahy snorted as Teddy knocked the wind from him and he toppled backward into two-right, crashing into dead bodies. He fired again, the flash of light illuminating for a split second Teddy's way of escape. He set off for the stairs even as the bullet ricocheted through the arched hallway. And he would've made it cleanly, too, had he not pitched headlong over the body of the stricken Vicar. Clancy hit the floor solidly, did a forward roll and was up again, scrambling toward the stairs. He scuttled upward, blasting open the doors with Cudahy's heavy footsteps on the stairs mere seconds behind him. Tearing through the churchyard, he hurdled small headstones and sidestepped others, the killer relentless in pursuit. As he burst through the cemetery entrance gates and turned onto Mary's Lane, he heard an automobile screech to a halt in front of St. Michan's as whistles blew. The police were joining the chase! But he couldn't stop now; he had to keep running until the cops overtook them. He might be caught, but the Book would be safe.

Evening strollers dove into alleyways and storefronts as Teddy blew past them, Cudahy some thirty yards behind, trying to line up a shot. Every time he was about to fire, Teddy would turn a corner. As he made his way down Capel Street toward the river, Cudahy squeezed off a round, but his arm's bouncing motion made him fire high, and a store window shattered close to Teddy's ear, shards of glass slicing his face. The river came into view as Clancy began to tire. He could not believe that Cudahy was not exhausted, and Teddy would have lost him had the heavy book not been bouncing wildly upon his back.

Clancy and Cudahy bounded up the arched walkway of Ha'penny Bridge as two police cars came roaring up Ormond Quay from opposite directions, sealing their rear. As Teddy labored to the crest of the bridge he could see a lorry parked at the other end, a line of police already kneeling military-style, rifles trained on the running men. He turned and looked over his shoulder just as Cudahy pulled the trigger one last time. A searing pain pierced him underneath the right shoulder blade and spun him around violently, reflex action causing him to drop the sack to the pavement before he toppled over the railing. The last thing he remembered before he plunged into the Liffey's rushing current was the volley of rifles that caught Cudahy in a deadly crossfire and reduced him to a bleeding heap.

*   *   *   *

As the air stilled an inspector from Scotland Yard, attired in a stylish summer suit, knelt over the dead man, surrounded by Irish police with still-smoking guns. They turned their attention to the dark waters.

"See anything?" the Englishman asked no one in particular.

"Went under like a stone, he did," answered a mustachioed sergeant.

"Notify headquarters," said the impeccably dressed detective in his clipped London accent. "The Book of Kells was successfully recovered. A gunman was pursued and killed. Another man, identity unknown, was shot and plunged into the river. We must position men in the areas between here and the harbor where things usually wash up."

"An' if nobody turns up?" questioned the sergeant, barely masking his annoyance at the British inspector.

"Then we'll drag the river." He reached into the dead man's coat and retrieved a tattered wallet. "Hopefully, we'll find out just who Mr. Brendan Cudahy was so bloody intent on shooting."

Chapter Twenty-Six

Boston

The pitcher, hands thrust deeply into his trouser pockets, dejectedly left the clubhouse and shuffled out of the players' entrance, eyes downcast. He felt terribly embarrassed. He could still hear the crack of Ruth's grand slam home run exploding off his bat. *Mother of God* he thought, *it must have gone a mile.*

He had just crossed the street from Fenway to a row of storefronts when two large men approached him. They appeared to be in their late thirties and wore turtleneck sweaters and caps similar to those of the Aran fishermen back home. "Clancy? Martin Clancy?" said the one on the left through a flaming red beard.

"Sorry boys, no autographs today," mumbled the right-hander.

The two men chuckled. "No, no," said the other one genially. "We don't want an autograph, Martin. We're friends of yer uncle!"

Martin suddenly brightened. "Uncle Ted? You know Ted Clancy?"

"Aye," said the one on the left, extending his hand, "we know him quite well."

Clancy readily offered his hand in friendship, and was taken completely off guard when the man jerked him forward and thrust a knee into his groin. The tired pitcher gasped and doubled over in pain as his two assailants quickly bundled him into a dark, narrow alley between the stores. They threw him against the wall, breaking his nose. Then they beat him senseless.

Minutes later, the sweating thugs surveyed their handiwork. "Now the finishing touch," said the bearded one, flicking open a switchblade. Its razor-sharp edge caught muted light. "This is for yer dear Uncle Teddy," he whispered, and went to work.

*   *   *   *

Martin regained consciousness the next morning, coming out of his deep, sedated sleep in stages. When he opened his eyes, he saw nothing but white. For a second he thought he was dead, but then his eyes focused and he realized that he was in a hospital room.

"Praise God, he's with us," said a familiar voice.

Clancy turned his head ever so slightly toward the sound. The pain in his neck was excruciating, and he could hardly breathe. He was relieved to find Monsignor Garvey, Lefty, and Bill Carrigan at his bedside. He forced himself to say, "What happened?"

"Easy now," said Lefty. "Marty, it looks like you got jumped on the way home yesterday. The owner of a delicatessen found you in the alley behind his place around seven last night. He called the cops and they rushed you here."

"Who—"

"We don't know who did this to you, kid, but we'll find the bastards," snarled Carrigan.

"Lots of pain," whispered the young pitcher.

"They broke you up pretty good, Marty," said Cremins, whose lip was quivering. "Try not to move too much."

"What'd they look like, lad?" asked Garvey.

Martin thought hard. His head was pounding. "Don't remember. Everything blank."

The doctor came in, a small, wiry man with a pinched face. "Ah, he's awakened. Good, good!" He took Martin's pulse. "For a while there it was precarious."

"Praise God," repeated the clergyman.

"All right, gentlemen," said the doctor. "There will be plenty of time to visit with Mr. Clancy tomorrow. You've been here for hours. Why don't you go home and get some sleep?" The men were indeed exhausted after their all-night vigil.

"See you later, after the game," whispered Lefty. "Hang in there,

157

Marty."

"That goes double for me, kid," said the manager, whose eyes were teary. "I'll be by with Mr. Quinn later. And don't worry; the club is taking care of everything."

"I'll say a mass for you today, son," offered the monsignor. "You'll be just fine, with the grace of God."

They left the room with the doctor in tow. He clicked the door closed behind them and followed them to a waiting room. "Is he gonna be all right?" asked Lefty expectantly.

"Yes, I believe so," said the physician calmly. "We're lucky he's with us. However, the men who attacked him did a considerable amount of damage. Besides a broken nose, he suffered a severe concussion. He has a fractured cheekbone and two cracked ribs. There was some internal bleeding. And then there's his hand. Terrible damage was done, I'm afraid."

"Will he ever be able to pitch again?" asked Carrigan.

"Not with that hand. You see, whomever it was that got hold of him knew exactly what he wanted to do. The tendons of the index, middle and ring fingers were severed with a sharp instrument. It took three hours of surgery just to sew the fingers back on. They were literally hanging by a thread. I'm sorry, gentlemen."

Lefty sank into a chair. Carrigan cursed and stared out the window.

The doctor furrowed his brow. "One thing is strange, though. In his delirium, he kept mumbling something about an Uncle Teddy being careful or some such thing. Mean anything to you?"

The three visitors shook their heads, but Garvey felt a chill go up his spine. The good monsignor spent the night deep in prayer, polishing off a bottle of Bushmills in the process.

Chapter Twenty-Seven

Dublin

No body was ever found. After a week of dragging the Liffey from Ha'penny Bridge to Dublin Harbor, the search was abandoned. Vicar Stafford, the only man who could have shed some light on the case, lapsed into a coma and died a week later. The Book of Kells was returned intact to Trinity College, where a more protective safe was employed in the future. The Book's theft and subsequent rescue were never revealed to the public.

*   *   *   *

A few days after the body of Brendan Cudahy was interred in a plot alongside his father, Mike Clancy received a letter, postdated July 28 with no return address that contained the princely sum of 200 pounds—roughly what Mike hoped to earn in half a year's work. Although he could not be sure, the printing on the envelope could have been his brother's. But what would that good-for-nothing be doing sending him money?

*   *   *   *

On that fateful day in 1927 when Martin Clancy took the mound at Fenway Park to do battle with the hated Yankees, a young man with curly black hair and a full beard knocked on the front door of the residence hall of the Christian Brothers on the backward, windswept island of Newfoundland. He hunched his shoulders against a keening gale that was blowing in off the water. After an interminable wait, an elderly, craggy-faced man in full cassock answered the door. "Come in, me son, yer soaked!" he exclaimed in a thick Irish brogue.

Once inside the young man stood dripping on the slate floor. In the next room, he could smell a fire and heard the sounds of mirthful conversation.

"Now then," said the old man, "what brings you to this godforsaken outpost of civilization, and where have you come from?"

"Well, Brother," said the traveler, "me name's Ted Clancy, and I hail from Cashel in County Tipperary. I've come here to join the order of the Christian Brothers."

"The dickens you say!" cried the old man. "All the way from Cashel to help us spread the word and educate the poor lads of Newfoundland. But why?"

Teddy reached into his back pocket and produced a tattered, waterlogged book. "I had the opportunity to learn about the Christian Brothers order, sir, and it seems a very worthwhile way to spend one's life. I've been told a time or two that I've a penchant for helping others, and I was informed that this area is dearly in need of such help."

"That it is, lad, that it is," mused the old man. "But why not do yer good back in Ireland? This is a lonely place, far removed from what one would call the beaten path."

Teddy smiled. "Perhaps, sir," he replied, "I need to find me own path."

The old man's eyes twinkled. "Well said!" He extended his hand and shook Teddy's warmly. "Come inside and let's have a cup of tea."

Epilogue

Boston, Massachusetts—September 1997

Seven men, their collars turned up against a raw, misty rain, stood on the fringe of the pitcher's mound in the empty ballpark as a baby-faced Catholic priest offered the Prayers for the Dead. A hole about eight inches wide and four feet deep had been bored straight down through the mound to accommodate the brass urn Ted Williams held to his chest. Besides Williams, his son and the priest, Carl Yastrzemski, Roger Clemens, Dom D'Ambrosio and a very old man murmured prayers and bowed their heads.

D'Ambrosio had been notified by John Harrington himself that Clancy wanted him at his funeral, whenever that might be. He wore his usher's outfit in tribute. Yaz had flown up from a baseball card show on Long Island where he was signing autographs, and Clemens had taken the redeye on his travel day with the Blue Jays scant moments after having landed with the team in Anaheim. "Never thought the old boy'd die," he whispered to Yastrzemski in his Texas twang. "What was he, a hunnerd?"

"Pretty near," muttered Yaz. He smiled thinly.

The brief service concluded, the priest excused himself, and the mourners repaired to the locker room in the ballpark's bowels, where the clubhouse man had laid out coffee, cake, and a bottle of brandy.

The old-timer, who'd hung back as the group had made their way inside, now stood apart with a steaming cup of coffee, inspecting a new pile of baseball bats, lost in thought. Suddenly, Ted Williams broke away from the others and came over, leaning on his cane. "Don't tell me

161

you're Lefty Cremins," he said with a raised eyebrow.

"Nobody's called me that in years," he replied. "One and the same, and I sure know who you are." He extended a weathered hand in greeting.

"Christ almighty, Clancy told me so much about you. Sorry, but I thought you were dead."

Cremins threw back his head and laughed, a raucous, tinny cackle that got everyone's attention. "Nah, I'm still kicking. Too bad about Marty, though. I'll miss him. Not too many of the old guys left from my day."

As the two spoke, the others sidled over and listened in, as if Cremins was a missing piece to the puzzle they constituted this day. "What I never got," continued Williams, "was how Clancy went from being a ballplayer to becoming an usher. I thought after what happened to him he'd say screw baseball, you know?"

Cremins cleared his throat, realizing he now had an audience. "Well, it's like this. After he got cut up he couldn't stand to face any of the guys, including me. When he recovered, he checked out of the hospital and disappeared. He knocked around Boston, doing odd jobs. Then he found steady work at a meatpacking plant in the North End, which he hated. Real nasty work."

"How did you learn this?" asked Yastrzemski.

"He wrote to me eventually. Somehow he found out I'd gone back home, for good. See, in '28 Quinn sent me a pitiful contract. He even wanted me to start the season in Wilkes-Barre again. No way was I doing that, so I quit. Gave it up, just like that. Marty wasn't happy with my decision but he respected it, and we continued to correspond off and on over the years.

"Anyway, Marty was really depressed. I mean, the poor guy, he couldn't even join the service during the second war because of his hand. He was living in a one-room cold water flat near Fenway, drinking a lot and feeling sorry for himself. Then, he told me, one day he was walking home from work, and there was a game going on at the ballpark; he heard the crowd buzzing and smelled those roasted peanuts and hot dogs, and it was like magic. He quit his job the next day, marched into the new owner's office—that was Mr. Yawkey—told him his story, and begged him for a job, which he got. You know, Mr. Yawkey became like a second father to him, even though their age difference wasn't that great. The boss couldn't believe his dedication. The guy never missed a game in fifty years. Never! Much later, when they were getting on in years, Marty half-jokingly mentioned being buried at Fenway and Yawkey said, 'Consider it done.' He was determined that Marty's wish would be carried out, no matter what. When he sold the club, one of the stipulations was that whoever owned the club down the road would honor this request. As you can see, Mr. Harrington was only carrying out Mr. Yawkey's wish.

"Well, after he left Yawkey's office that first day he went right over to St. Catherine's Church and got old Monsignor Garvey to hire him on as a caretaker. Let's face it; the old guy owed him one. The job came with an apartment in the rectory basement that suited his needs perfectly. Look, he had no family. He told me about some lady friends over the years, and that he was actually in love once, but he never felt the urge to marry. The Red Sox and the Church were all the family he needed.

"Marty wanted us here because he saw something special in each of us, I guess. You, of course, Mr. Williams, were a perfectionist in your craft, and you loved the game as he did. Mr. Yastrzemski, he admired the way you won the Triple Crown and carried the ballclub on your back in '67 to get to the World Series, which was his favorite. Mr. Clemens, he so enjoyed to watch you throw that fastball, oh yes. He told me he would have dreams of pitching after every start you made, and he'd wake from those dreams with his arm tingling. But he worried about you, felt that your desire for greatness would consume you. Guess he was wrong on that one." He turned to Dom. "And Mr. D'Ambrosio, you weren't a ballplayer, but Marty saw you as someone lost in the woods, his wayward son, if you will. He wanted you to feel the same way he did about baseball." He paused and placed his coffee cup on the clubhouse table. "I'm here because I was his best friend in the world, except maybe for his Uncle Ted. Funny how he never held a grudge against the man for what happened, although holding grudges wouldn't be Marty's way, anyway."

"What happened to the uncle?" asked John Henry Williams. "Did he ever hear from him again?"

"Yeah, just once," said Cremins, reaching into his pocket. "I was at Marty's apartment this morning. What little he left, he left to me." He smiled affectionately.

"Around 1940 a letter came to Monsignor Garvey's office, addressed to Marty. No return address, just an explanation of what had happened in his uncle's life, and an apology. And this piece of paper with a poem on it, which Marty kept in his Bible. Want to hear it?"

"Yes, please," said Clemens.

Cremins carefully unfolded the crumbling yellowed paper and held it at arm's length. After clearing his throat again, he read aloud:

> "So we'll go no more a-roving
> So late into the night,
> Though the heart be still as loving,
> And the moon be still as bright.
>
> For the sword outweighs its sheath,
> And the soul wears out the breast,
> And the heart must pause to breathe,
> And love itself have rest.
>
> Though the night is made for loving,
> And the day returns too soon
> Yet we'll go no more a-roving
> By the light of the moon."

He looked up, his pale eyes watery. "That's it, then, gentlemen."

"Yes," added Dom, "and God bless all here."

Author's Note

To call this book a labor of love would be an understatement. It was originally written some 25 years ago, as a Valentine's Day present for my wife Maria. I am happy to report that she is still my bride and constant proofreader.

The parts that take place in Ireland, primarily in Cashel and Dublin, were researched thoroughly, including multiple visits to the sites mentioned. If you are ever in the Emerald Isle, don't forego a trip to the hometown of Martin Clancy and the Rock of Cashel. You will never forget it. And, of course, visits to Trinity College to view the actual Book of Kells, and the eerily interesting St. Michan's Church, are a must. If there was ever a hauntingly evocative place that could inspire a writer more than Ireland, I haven't found it.

As far as the baseball end of things, I owe the accuracy and realism of the 1927 baseball season events depicted here to the two men mentioned in my dedication.

Robert Creamer was, in addition to the Christian Brothers at Iona College, one of my greatest writing mentors. In addition to being the Senior Editor of *Sports Illustrated* for many years, he also became famous as a first-class baseball biographer. Bob's 1974 portrait of Babe Ruth, entitled *Babe: The Legend Comes to Life*, is still the gold standard for Ruth retrospectives. During the period of our friendship and collaboration in his later years, Bob took the time and interest to examine this manuscript for historical accuracy, especially the exploits of the 1927 "Murderer's Row" Yankees and their iconic star, George Herman Ruth. But more than that, he encouraged me as a writer and gave me the impetus to see this project through. It has taken a while, but somewhere I know Bob is smiling.

When I first met Lefty Cremins, he was in his late 80s and one of the oldest surviving major leaguers. Being from my hometown of Pelham, New York, he was known to all as a dedicated longtime village official and youth boxing coach. I cherish the moments we sat in his cluttered living room amidst his various awards, memorabilia and artwork, while he regaled me with stories of his "cup of coffee" with the Red Sox in 1927, in which he got to make the "grand tour" of the American League and, incredibly, face Ruth and the Yankees as a pitcher. Bob's stories of the Bambino, Lou Gehrig, and Ty Cobb were the basis for the adventures of the young Lefty and the fictional Martin Clancy. Bob died in 2004 at the ripe old age of 98, and I can't think of anyone who led a fuller life.

The Rovers: A Tale of Fenway isn't just a story about baseball and its continuum through the years; it is a story about the human condition and the innate desire of man to become something more than what he is. I think Teddy and Martin did just that — thanks to, as in the case of this humble writer, the help and caring of those around him.

Play Ball!
Paul Ferrante, 2016

About The Author

Paul Ferrante is originally from the Bronx and grew up in the town of Pelham, NY. He received his undergraduate and Master's degrees in English from Iona College, where he was also a halfback on the Gaels' undefeated 1977 football team. Paul has been an award-winning secondary school English teacher and coach for over 35 years, as well as a columnist for *Sports Collector's Digest* since 1993 on the subject of baseball ballpark history. Many of his works can be found in the archives of the National Baseball Hall of Fame in Cooperstown, NY. His writings have led to numerous radio and television appearances related to baseball history. He is the author of the popular *T.J. Jackson Mysteries* (Young Adult) series, published by Fire & Ice, the Young Adult imprint of Melange Books, LLC. *The Rovers: A Tale of Fenway* is his first adult novel.

Paul lives in Connecticut and Florida with his wife Maria and daughter Caroline, a film director/screenwriter.

Please visit Paul's website: **www.paulferranteauthor.com** for information on all his writing, including the *T.J. Jackson Mysteries*. Also visit **www.facebook.com/TJJacksonmysteries**.

The T.J. Jackson Mysteries

Last Ghost at Gettysburg
Spirits of the Pirate House
Roberto's Return
Curse of the Fairfield Witch